SHE

S.E. Walker

PublishAmerica
Baltimore

First printing

PublishAmerica has allowed this work to remain exactly as the author intended, verbatim, without editorial input.

ISBN: 1-60441-648-3
PUBLISHED BY PUBLISHAMERICA, LLLP
www.publishamerica.com
Baltimore

Printed in the United States of America

Dedicated to all the women
who are enduring abuse today
To those who found their way out
And to those who gave their lives for love

SHE

S.E. Walker

TABLE OF CONTENTS

Chapter 1

I can do this, I can do this, I can do this, she assured herself as the scent of sweat, cigarette smoke and alcohol drowned her. If she repeated it often enough, maybe her brain would believe it, though the knotting in her stomach warned that her body did not agree. Her belly clenched as if preparing to send her dinner of reheated leftovers north again. He was back and he was horny. She turned away from his open-mouthed kiss though a similar kiss had woken her just seconds before. Half expecting this all evening, she'd still been caught off guard and asleep.

The shaft of light streaming through a two-inch wide opening in the curtains across the room caught her attention. That peachy-pink glow drew her mind away from her body, away from the man groping one breast while suckling at the other. That light kept her from screaming and clawing for escape as he shifted to lie over her, trapping her beneath his sticky, sweat-covered body. This was, after all, her job. Every minute or so he slid a hand into the apex of her thighs to judge how her body was reacting to his efforts at foreplay. He wanted her panting and moaning, though that was the last thing she felt. She'd rather roll over and go back to the sleep she'd been ripped from, but that was not to be. At least, not for a few more minutes.

Taking a breath, she shifted into the act of enjoying his sexual performance. Anything to move this production along. Her moaning with faked passion should win her an award for best actress in a sex scene somewhere in the world. If only someone could witness this moment. It always surprised her that he never realized her passion was a ruse. She had been pretending for so many years she could not remember what a real orgasm felt like.

I can do this, I can do this, I can do this. He shifted and slid into her with his patented groan of passion. Then he forced her head around so he could kiss her again. He paused once he was fully seated in her. Then he began to piston in and out, changing positions and tempos every few strokes. She closed her eyes so he would not see the contempt she was feeling. Rolling her face away from his, she took a breath of air that wasn't tainted with his cigarette smoke and whiskey breath. Gritting her teeth to keep the scream of rage inside, she concentrated on her performance. All the while she prayed he would finish before she threw up.

Two minutes later he growled deep in his throat and stiffened for a few endless seconds. He collapsed so heavily on her chest, she could not take a breath, bar tainted or otherwise. When she would have bucked him off or blacked out from lack of oxygen, he jerked his shriveling manhood from her core. He rolled onto his back with a sigh of satisfaction.

"Wow, that was great. Did you get yours?" his words slurred together as he reached out and patted her left breast.

Her lips curled into a shadow of a smile as she murmured a soft "uh huh."

He rolled from the bed without another glance in her direction. He'd gotten what he wanted, now for more important matters. "Dibbies on the bathroom."

As soon as he was out of sight behind the bathroom door, she shivered. Swallowing hard, she blinked away the tears that threatened to expose the extent of her misery. Reaching to the floor on her side of the bed, she brushed her hand against the industrial-grade, oatmeal-colored Berber carpet they'd installed last year. She snatched up the first bit of clothing her fingers touched. She had to wipe away the still warm evidence of his passion that felt like acid burning her skin. She pushed herself to a sitting position, no longer worried about leaving a wet spot in the bed. Using the back of the fingers of her left hand, she brushed at her cheek, wiping away two tears that slipped past the locked iron gate that guarded her heart and emotions.

Get a grip. He'll be back in another minute. She forced the misery down further even though he would not notice. These days he never acknowledged her tears. Not after hurtful words at dinner, not during an emotionally touching movie, not even when they had sex. Her tears were not important to him. Nothing about her was important as long as she did her job and kept him happy.

The bathroom door opened and he appeared, scratching at his butt with one hand, his ear with the other. "I'm beat. How about you?"

"Yeah," she whispered her voice hoarse from keeping emotion under control, "exhausted."

As he crawled into the bed on the right side, she rose from the left. He was tired, sexually satisfied and drunk, but she kept her face averted anyway. She did not want him to see her pain, her disgust. He might ask what was wrong and she would have to lie. Again. Over the years, she had misrepresented the truth with him so much sometimes she wasn't sure herself what was real and was a lie. Tonight, however, her emotions were too close to the surface and shredding fast. She could not fabricate a story as to why her face was wet. She'd rather scream in anger or in agony, but that would lead to more questions she did not have answers to right now.

Once behind the safety of the bathroom door, she collapsed onto the toilet. He would not bother her in here. It was one of the unwritten rules of their marriage. The bathroom was off limits if the door was closed. She was safe for a few minutes. Letting go of the diamond hard control she had developed, she allowed herself the luxury of silent tears. Maybe by releasing a few now, the pressure behind her eyes would ease.

I cannot do this any more. I have to change. I am going to change. I cannot keep living like this.

Sniffing and still blinded by her tears, she pulled a clean washcloth from the stack in the linen closet. Running the hot water into the sink, she wet the cloth and wiped dried spittle from her cheeks, neck, breasts and body. As she removed the evidence of sex, she pushed down the ball of anger, hatred and self-pity that swelled in her chest.

She took another moment to brush her teeth and then comb the tangles from the auburn hair that hung to her waist in a waterfall of straightness. He thought the style suited her. She thought she looked like a teenybopper.

Looking into the mirror, she met her own gaze, but could only study her reflection for a few seconds before dropping her focus to the sink. The eyes looking back at her had always been brown, but when had they turned the color of dried dog shit? No sparkle, no life, just dull, dull brown with flat black pupils. Her normally ivory skin was as pale as the soft cotton white wall behind her, except for the rosy beard burn around her chin and breasts. Turning out the light, paused to pull close the invisible cloak of calm she always wore around him. With a deep breath, she opened the bathroom door.

That calm exterior was an illusion he never bothered to see beyond to the blaze of emotion that raged behind her clever façade. He always thought she was placid, calm, agreeable in a way that appealed to him. In truth she held a firestorm secreted behind a firewall. She was not sure how much longer she would be able to keep those fiery feelings under control, though she was terrified of releasing them. She could not predict what might happen if she let herself go. Would she beat him to death with a wooden spoon or cry herself into a coma?

As she stepped into the darkened bedroom, rhythmic grunting snores met her. She was safe. She would not have to call up her ever-expanding acting skills tonight. Crossing the room, she stood and watched her husband sleep in peaceful ignorance.

* * * * *

Five days later, she looked across the table and the skin between her shoulders crawled. She wanted to bring them up as close to her ears as possible and then down back down again to ease the feeling, but did not. It wouldn't help. Nothing ever did.

She looked past the overcooked meatloaf with BBQ sauce smeared over the top, the lumpy mashed potatoes and the mushy canned corn at the man she had vowed to spend the rest of her life with. For the first time in months she really looked at him. In a momentary flash of genius-like insight she realized he would never change. He was content, even happy, with meatloaf Thursdays and spaghetti Mondays and sex on alternate Saturday nights after he had drinks with the boys down at the Sheraton. To him life was fine, comfortable and predictable, just the way he liked it. He did not see that she was drowning in sadness.

Only once had she tried to change the menu, hoping to inject a little sparkle and zip into their meals. She still cringed at the memory of that evening.

* * * * *

"What is this crap?" he demanded when she set the Pyrex French White casserole dish on the table between their plates. "That's not spaghetti."

"This is seafood Alfredo," she said.

"It's Monday, spaghetti night. This isn't spaghetti," he persisted.

"Won't you at least taste this? I thought we could try something different," she said, her happiness at accomplishing the complicated recipe evaporating in the heat of his darkening expression.

"I like knowing what's for dinner. That way I can prepare myself for your cooking. I was all set for spaghetti with meat sauce. You make that so well."

She was ready to throw the meal away and start over. The thought of hamburger fried up and mixed into canned spaghetti sauce then poured over spaghetti turned her stomach. She blinked several times to keep the rising tears from falling. Her earlier joy was gone, replaced by a headache and queasy stomach. After allowing him to serve himself a large helping, she took a single spoonful. He cleaned his plate, twice, while she picked at the noodles and shrimp on her own plate.

"That was pretty good, I guess," Matthew admitted as he wiped his lips on his napkin. "Maybe you can fix it the next time my folks come to dinner. But next Monday, make spaghetti."

* * * * *

The memory caused sadness to bubble up and swamped her. Dreading a lifetime of Thursday meatloaf dinners and a life revolving around Matthew's every want, need and demand, her racing thoughts of unhappiness crystallized into one single, mind-blowing conclusion.

I cannot do this anymore. I have got to get out.

"Did you say something?" Matthew looked up from mixing the last of the canned corn into his third helping of mashed potatoes. The combination turned her stomach, but that was how he ate those vegetables, mixed together with lots of butter, salt and pepper.

She had not spoken her thoughts aloud, had she? "I didn't say anything," she murmured, crossing the fingers of her left hand that lay in her lap. The childhood belief of canceling out a lie did little to make her feel better. She had been lying for so long would ever overcome them all?

"Uh huh. Oh yeah, I'm going fishing tomorrow with the boys," Matthew announced as casually as he did the weather forecast. Pushing from his chair, he left his dishes where they were and headed for the bedroom.

Her eyes widened, but she did not speak. Thank God was her first thought, but she swallowed those words as she followed him.

She watched as he packed his clothes. Tears pressed against the back of her eyelids. Though she looked forward to the time alone, it hurt that he was free to jump in his car and take off with his fishing buddies at a moment's notice and she was trapped in the house. As he piled bags by the back door, he looked at her when she sniffed twice in rapid succession.

"What's up with you?"

"Nothing. Go, have a great weekend," she said, not able to keep the bitterness out of her voice. She could not keep the single tear from slipping down her cheek.

"Why are you crying? You gonna miss me that much? If you don't want me to go say so," he said, his tone shifting from surprised to accusatory to put out in three sentences.

"Go."

"So why are you crying?"

"I just wish I could take off spur of the moment for a weekend away," she said after swallowing hard.

I wish I could pack my bags and leave and never come back. I wish I would never have to have another one of these unwinnable conversations with you.

"So go. I'm not stopping you. You keep talking about spending a weekend at that bed and breakfast in Beaufort. What's stopping you?"

"It costs money to go to a bed and breakfast. I don't have any money. You've squirreled it all away," she lashed out. Sniffing again, she gave up the battle to hide her tears. The pressure behind her eyes was too great.

It did not matter. If tears could make him feel guilty, she would use them, but nothing would change him. Wasn't there a country song called "Men Don't Change"?

"I suppose I could foot the bill if you want to go away for a weekend sometime. Let me know and I'll give you some money," Matthew said in his conciliatory, patient father voice. He pulled her to him for a one-armed hug as if that would make everything all right.

She closed her eyes and gritted her teeth, working hard not to shudder at his touch. If only he would hug her properly, wrap both arms around her and pull her tight to his chest. Maybe then she would feel loved. She had not been wrapped in loving, supportive arms since her mother had died two years before. Would she ever feel a warm, protective embrace again? Or was she forever sentenced to one-armed hugs and no-lip kisses that almost connected with her skin before they were over?

Matthew patted her shoulder, emphasizing the fact that he no longer saw her as a sexual being. She could have been any woman on Earth. His interest in her only rose after he had been out drinking with the boys. She would worry that he was having an affair, but he had admitted more than once to being scared spitless that he might catch AIDS or syphilis or some other sexually transmitted disease. It was the only reason she had not accused him of such a thing before now.

He did not have the same concern. "You would never step out on me," he'd told her on more than one occasion. "No man would have you. Men want a good-looking woman who is sure of her sexuality and knows how to play. You strike out on all counts. You're a plain, pudgy mouse of a woman who's afraid of her own shadow. Aren't I lucky that you're all mine?"

She never responded to his "discussions" of the problems in their marriage. Pointing out his faults when he demanded she tell him how she felt just earned her more insults, more putdowns, more criticisms. He did not care what she thought of him. He claimed to have nothing that needed changing. She, on the other hand, needed to change everything.

* * * * *

Friday morning Matthew left for work after patting her shoulder and brushing a kiss near her lips as he did every weekday morning. "Have dinner ready when I get home, okay? We want to get out on the river before dark."

"Yeah, sure," she said following him as far as the back door. Closing the door behind him, she flipped the deadbolt, then turned and leaned against it. "Of course your dinner will be ready when you get home. Isn't it always?" With a deep breath, she pushed away from the door and headed to the bedroom. Time to get her own day started.

She had just finished making the bed when tears started to fall. Instead of moving on to the next chore, she crawled onto the queen-size bed she had just finished making and curled into a ball.

The tears came from deep in her center. They rendered her immobile. The sound of sobbing filled the otherwise silent house. She was thirty-four years old, but felt a hundred and four. She could count her friends on one hand and still have fingers left over. Matthew had made her dependent on him for everything.

What's happened to me? I used to be creative and ambitious and happy. When did I become Matthew's floor mat? What happened to the backbone and fiery spirit that intimidated the boys back when I was in high school and college?

Lying on the bed, she forced herself to look back at the last ten years of her life.

Chapter 2

It seemed like it was just yesterday, not nearly eleven years before.

"Happy birthday toooo yooouuuuu." What had begun as a duet at their table in the corner of the room had become a full bar, four-part harmony chorus by the last line of the traditional birthday song.

She raised her half-full glass of white wine in salute to the room. "Thank you," she said, her smile wide. Her cheeks burned bright from the attention. Never before had twenty or so men stare at her all at one time. The older ones smiled while some of the younger men looked like wolves checking out their next meal.

Setting her glass down, she pushed back from the table, "Time to take a short break," she told her the two women grinning at her.

"You can't leave now!" Sharon Brackett said. "You just got the attention of the entire bar. When the band starts playing, they'll be lining up for a dance with the birthday girl."

"I'm not leaving, I'm going to recycle that first glass of wine. You want to come with me?"

"I do," Loretta Brown said, rising from her chair as well. "Otherwise you might try to crawl out the bathroom window or slip out the back door instead of coming back for another drink."

She had to smile. These two women, her co-workers, were trying to make her 23rd birthday memorable. Though they were determined to keep her here, all she wanted was to go home to her bed. It had been a long Friday at the end of a very long week.

Working in a pediatrician's office during flu season meant ten and twelve-hour days, for the office staff as well as the doctor and his two nurses. Thankfully the week was over and she had nothing planned but a trip to the Laundromat early tomorrow morning and church on Sunday.

"Excuse me, I was wondering if I could have the next dance," a man stepped between her and the path to the ladies' room. He was tall and attractive with smiling eyes and dirty-blonde hair that was beginning to show signs of thinning across the front. In a few years his hairline would be receding and he would be cutting his hair shorter and shorter as was the current trend among men.

He had a friendly air about him, so she stammered, "Um, sure. As soon as I get back."

The stranger nodded, then took a step to his left to allow her to pass. Loretta followed close behind. The crowd was growing fast as the serious party people arrived just before nine o'clock to avoid the cover charge that went into effect then. Nine o'clock was also when the DJ packed up his equipment and a live band took over until closing time.

"He's cute," Loretta said with a giggle that proved two margaritas were too much for this mother of three who rarely had a chance to get out. "Don't let him get away," she instructed as they stepped into the restroom.

"It's just a dance," she said.

"A lifetime together begins with a dance. Just a dance leads to dinner, then a movie and more dancing. Before you know it you'll be setting up house together and picking out baby names."

"You're drunk and silly," she said, not sure how else to get Loretta to shut up.

"Yeah, ain't it great?" Loretta said, giggling again. "It's been a long time since I've had more than one drink in an evening. We need to do this more often. Like every Friday after work."

"And what would Karl say about that?" she asked, referring to Loretta's husband and the father of their three children.

"If it gets him a little action when I get home he'd be all for it. Come on, let's get you back to that hunky stranger," Loretta said, pushing her through the restroom door and back into the bar. The lights were dimmer when they emerged. It took a few seconds for their eyes to adjust. When she could look around without squinting, she was surprised to find someone standing right beside her.

"Ready for that dance?" he asked, placing his hand in the center of her back.

"Uh, sure," she said. No man had ever waited outside the ladies room for her before. Had he heard their conversation? Or had there been too much noise coming from the main room for him to hear Loretta's instructions?

He guided her to the dance floor that was about forty feet square and empty for the moment. He waved at the DJ who nodded, then hit a button. Immediately Celine Dion began to sing "My Heart Will Go On" from the Titanic movie. He pulled her close and held her. "I'm Matthew," he said. "Matthew Morgan." His breath was minty fresh and he smelled of clean clothes and strong, almost overpowering, cologne.

Instead of answering, she wondered if she should ease back so there was an inch or two of space between them. They were strangers, but his hold was nice, comforting, so she stayed where she was. Less than thirty seconds after the music began they were joined by several other couples. They had to dance in smaller and smaller circles until they were merely turning circles.

When the song ended, Matthew led the way back to her table. They found two glasses of white wine and a pink envelope with her name on it, but the two women were nowhere in sight. Even their purses and coats were gone.

"Looks like you've been abandoned," Matthew said, holding her chair out for her. Once she was seated, he settled into the one next to her

"I guess that means the party is over," she said, slipping the pink envelope into the back pocket of her slacks without looking at it. She did not want to open what she knew would be a risqué card in front of this stranger.

"Just because they left doesn't mean you have to go. Or is there someone waiting at home for you?"

She thought of her tiny studio apartment with the full size bed that was pulling at her, but shook her head. "No, no one at home," she admitted softly.

"Then stay. Dance with me. Talk with me," he said, his voice smooth and persuasive.

After debating for five seconds she nodded. "All right."

By the time the lights came up at closing time she was mesmerized by Matthew Morgan. Nine years older than she was, he was knowledgeable on many subjects, outspoken in his opinions and firm in his political views. He looked into her eyes when he talked and really seemed to listen when she spoke. His blue eyes were hypnotic. Or was that the effect of the wine? Was this her third or fourth glass? She kept her comments brief as the hurtful words of the last man she'd dated still rang through her memory.

"You're too overbearing, too bold and you talk too much," he had said as he slipped from the steakhouse booth. He stormed from the restaurant without a backward glance, leaving her to pay for dinner. She was so shocked by his comments she had not thought about how she was going to get the forty miles home until she walked out the front door of the restaurant and found that he had left her stranded. Thankfully Sharon had been home and willing to come and get her.

"I want to see you again," Matthew said as they walked out of the bar at closing time.

"I'd like that," she said, the hurts of past relationships fading under the warm glances he kept sending her way.

* * * * *

They had been dating for two months when Matthew called one Saturday afternoon to tell her they had been invited to a party that evening.

"What shall I wear?" she asked, still unsure of herself in this man's world. As a salesman for his father's company, he always dressed nice. For their trip to a Kinston Indians' baseball game he wore neatly pressed khaki slacks, Dockers and a three-button golf shirt. Was this a jeans and T-shirt party or a dress up type of gathering?

"Whatever you want to wear. You're a big girl. I should not have to tell you how to dress all the time," Matthew snapped at her. "I'll pick you up in half an hour." Click.

Matthew's abrupt conversation endings still caught her off guard, but that didn't bother her as much as his assumption that she could be ready in thirty minutes. She would have loved two hours to shower and primp and relax, but thirty minutes was all she had. Just enough time to dress and touch up her makeup.

After flipping through her closet twice and still not sure of herself, she finally decided middle of the road was the way to go. She would either be way underdressed or way overdressed, but at least she'd be comfortable. She pulled out a long denim skirt and a white cotton sweater. Then she looked at the floor.

"I really need to do some shopping," she muttered as she kicked through the small pile of shoes. "But what will I use for money to redo my entire wardrobe?" She decided on a pair of brown flats that were comfortable and yet classically dressy.

After dressing, she put on fresh makeup with a heavier hand that usual. She brushed her hair, then pulled one side back with a clip. "That's as good as its going to get," she told her reflection as a brisk knock sounded at her door.

Matthew did not comment on her appearance. He just took her hand and pulled out the door. "Come on, we're late."

Within minutes of their arrival, she wished she had passed on the invitation and stayed home. The gathering was a pig picking at a riverfront cottage. It was a ratty T-shirt and trashy jeans kind of party with beer flowing freely from three half kegs that were iced down in the back of a pickup.

Matthew held her hand until someone handed him a plastic cup of beer. He handed it to her then accepted a second one for himself. A few minutes later he drifted away to join a group of men looking at a jet ski that was grounded at the river's edge. She followed for a few steps, but stopped when the one of the other men looked at her as if she were intruding on some private male bonding ritual.

She turned around, but not knowing anyone other than Matthew, she felt lost. The women were gathered on and near the front porch of the house. She joined the group, but had nothing to contribute to their discussions of children, husbands and other friends. She plastered a smile on her lips and sipped at her beer trying not to make a face. She much preferred white wine or a strawberry margarita.

"Matthew's a good guy," a woman twice her age commented. "Are you two dating?" The woman swayed with the loud music coming from the house. She had been drinking for awhile.

"Yes," she answered.

"He's never brought a woman to our parties before. You two must have something special going on."

"I like to think so."

"Well, enjoy yourself," the woman said before wandering off again.

"Thanks," she replied, her soft voice lost amid the screaming guitars and pounding drums.

By the time the food was served, she had drunk more than

usual, but was still no closer to feeling comfortable with this crowd of down home, good old guys and gals. The men ignored her except for occasional glances of curiosity, as if wondering why Matthew had chosen her. The women kept their distance, some envious because she was dating Matthew; others seemed intimidated by her simple denim skirt and blouse.

Even during the dinner of barbecue pork pulled from the pig cooked in the trailer-size grill Matthew kept his distance. He talked and laughed with everyone but her, flirting with the ladies and joking inappropriately with the men. This was a side of him she had never seen before. A redneck male chauvinist who was treating her like the other men were treating their wives, like property and not partners. By the time the midsummer sun finally disappeared from view, she was ready to walk home. Especially when she saw couples disappearing into the house and bushes that edged two sides of the property.

Taking a deep breath, she approached Matthew. “I'd like to go home now,” she said, standing close enough to brush her chest against his arm. She ignored the other four men he was talking to.

“Home? The party's just starting. These things can go on all night,” Matthew replied, his voice slurring from too much beer.

“Maybe so, but I'm ready to go home now.”

“Here, drive yourself. Park it in your parking lot and leave the keys under the mat. I'll pick it up later,” Matthew pulled his key ring from his pocket and held them out between thumb and first finger.

As she reached for them, he opened his fingers and deliberately dropped them. She gritted her teeth, but did not say a word as she knelt and picked them up. Without another look in his direction, she turned, found the car and walked away. As she drove across the field, she checked the rearview mirror. Matthew stood alone, watching her go. He looked shocked, as if he could not believe she had left.

Driving away, she felt nonexistent, almost ghostlike. She had not expected to be the life of a party, but she had hoped that Matthew would have stayed with her out of respect for her as his guest and as the woman he claimed to be falling in love with. She'd never expected him to abandon her to a group of strangers.

She slowed as anger eased and pain bubbled up causing tears to prickle her eyes and overflow. She parked his car next to hers in the parking lot and left the driver's door unlocked. She slipped the key ring under the floor mat and walked away without a backward glance.

She had done what he asked, leaving the car where he wanted and how he wanted. She almost hoped someone would steal his prized sportscar. But that would never happen. She lived in a safe, quiet apartment complex where the residents valued privacy and crime was unheard of.

When she locked the door of her apartment that night, she expected never to hear from Matthew again. She would be sad for awhile, but maybe it was for the best. After a quick shower, two Aspirin and a large glass of water, she climbed into bed, curled into a ball and passed out. The three beers she had drunk overwhelmed her normally tee-totaling system.

Sunday morning she kept herself busy. She caught up on all the chores she ignored during the week. At some point during the morning Matthew's car disappeared from the parking lot. She discovered it was gone when she took the garbage out after a late lunch.

"He didn't even bother to say thank you," she murmured as she climbed into her car for a trip to the grocery store. "I guess that's the last I see of him." She was surprised at the deep sadness that washed over her. She had thought they were a match. She had thought he was the one. She had thought she was in love.

At work on Monday she was quiet, but dodged Loretta's questions about the reason. This was her pain. She did not want to share it with anyone else.

Just before her lunch break, Loretta nudged her out of her thoughts and nodded toward the front door. "Someone to see you."

She looked up and was surprised to see Matthew standing in the middle of the waiting room holding a vase full of roses.

"Hi," he said as he crossed the room. He set the flowers on the counter between them.

"What's this?" she asked, stepping to the left to look around the overly large display of blood red roses.

Matthew was not looking at her. He was checking out the rest of the room and the women who were watching this interplay with much interest and envy. "I was a jerk on Saturday. I'm sorry." He looked at her and she caught the shininess of tears in his eyes. Was he so sensitive that he would cry because he had hurt her?

The anger she had carried since Saturday dissipated like early morning river fog in the sunlight. "It's all right," she said.

"So you'll forgive me?"

"Yes, I forgive you. Thank you for the flowers. Now go away so I can get back to work," she said with a smile. She knew Elizabeth, the office manager, was frowning at her for having someone distract her from her duties. She could feel the heat of the woman's stare.

"Kiss me and I'll go," he said, leaning close. He reached out, wrapped one hand around her neck and pulled her forward. She had to go up on tiptoes to reach him across the wide desk of the reception area. Thirty seconds later he released her, turned without another word and left the building whistling.

She grabbed the flowers that teetered on the edge of the counter, then retreated to her desk. She was unable to stop grinning. He did care about her.

* * * * *

"Let's go for a drive," he suggested on a gray Saturday morning four months later as they headed to the New Bern Farmer's Market for some Saturday morning shopping.

"Okay," she said automatically as she did to anything he suggested.

She wished he had asked her about this before they were in the car and on their way. She would have changed her loafers for sneakers and grabbed a jacket. The beach was sure to be cooler and breezier than New Bern.

Matthew headed down Highway 70 to Atlantic Beach. By the time they reached the end of the island, the drizzle that had started in Havelock deepened until it was a steady downpour. Instead of having a picnic on the beach, Matthew circled the empty parking lot at Fort Macon State Park and headed down the island. When they reached Emerald Isle at the other end of the island, he pulled into the parking lot of the Sundowner Motel. He drove until they were as close to the beach as possible before he parked.

"Stay here, I'll be right back," he said as he climbed from the car. Ten minutes later he returned looking like a cat that had eaten a whole flock of canaries.

"Come on," he said after opening her door, "and bring that stuff," he waved toward the backseat. Then he jogged away again.

She struggled with the heavy picnic basket and wool stadium blanket. By the time she reached Matthew under the wide porch cover, she was soaked. He stood next to an open door. "Come on," he said, ushering her into the room.

"What are we doing here?" she asked as she stopped two steps inside the room. Though they'd made love, she wasn't prepared for an afternoon quickie. She was cold and wet and the picnic basket Matthew had packed was heavy.

Matthew crossed to the curtains on the other side of the room. With a dramatic pull on the cord, the curtains parted. This gave them an unobstructed view of the beach and ocean. "Since we can't have our picnic on the beach, we can at least look at the beach while we're eating," he said.

"How nice," she replied. Sometimes he could be the most

thoughtful man. She did not think about the other times when she wondered why she was dating him because he was not so thoughtful or kind. He had told her more than once they were fated to be together and nothing would separate them. Her curves fit his hollows, he would say.

They spread the stadium blanket on the floor, then ate lunch while watching the waves roll in. Once they finished Matthew pulled her close and gazed deep into her eyes. "You are so good for me," he said, brushing her hair back from her face. "Did you cut your hair?" he asked, a frown creasing his forehead.

"Just a trim," she said, surprised that he noticed. She had not changed the shoulder length bob since high school, only getting an inch trimmed every six weeks or so.

"Don't cut your hair anymore. Long hair is so much sexier," he said. He leaned close to brush a kiss across her lips. "Not that you need help being sexy, but you would look so great with long hair."

"Okay," she agreed without thinking about it. Her mind was fogging from the sexual magic his hands and lips were performing on her body. All he had to do was start kissing her and touching her and she would agree to anything he asked.

"Marry me," he breathed. He reached for the button at the waistband of her faded blue jeans.

His words barely registered. "Okay," she said the next time they came up for air with her jeans around her knees and her shirt shoved to her throat.

In seconds they were naked and lost in a frenzy of intense, fast-paced sex. Matthew peaked first and collapsed on her with a roaring groan of satisfaction.

She waited until he was in the bathroom before she reached down with two fingers and completed her climb to orgasm alone. It only took a few seconds to finish what had been so close, yet so far away. When she came down from that peak, she felt embarrassed and guilty though she could not explain why. It was not his fault she took longer to find orgasm than he did. She told herself she was just inexperienced and untrained. After all, he was only the third man she'd been with. It would get better, she assured herself.

When Matthew emerged from the closet-size bathroom, she couldn't look at him as she went in. When she came out after cleaning up, he had pulled on his boxer shorts and crawled into the bed. She pulled on her T-shirt and joined him. They cuddled and she fell asleep to the sound of rain beating on the windows and Matthew's soft snores.

She woke to Matthew exploring her body in a leisurely, relaxed manner. When he saw her eyes were open, he came over her and they made love again.

The rain ended just before full dark. She lounged on the bed, putting off dressing for a few more minutes. Matthew was half dressed. He was standing at the window staring out. Giving in to the deepening shadows, he turned on a lamp. She saw his reflection in the window and not the world beyond the glass.

His reflection was distorted, his expression unreadable. But he did not look happy. For some reason, she was reminded of her father, a man who had never seemed happy with his life or anyone around him. Nothing ever pleased him. She had learned early in life that when Daddy came home in a bad mood, it was best to stay small and silent and out of his way.

She jumped when Matthew turned and frowned at her. "Aren't you dressed yet? We need to get home," he said. "We have a lot to do if we're going to get married next week." He pulled his polo over his head at the same time he stepped into his Dockers. He missed the astonished look she sent his way.

"Next week?" she asked, still recovering from the shock of his proposal. "I can't pull a wedding together in a week. No one can. Especially with work and all."

"Don't you worry about anything except being the prettiest bride you can be. I'll take care of everything else," he said.

She scrambled for her clothes as his words sunk in. He would plan their wedding? In a week?

He had to be kidding. She'd never heard of a groom who

planned the biggest day of their lives. Men were supposed to tell their bride to do what she wanted. All he needed to know was where and when and what to wear. Other than that the groom stayed out of the way. If cornered, their favorite phrase was supposed to be "Whatever you want, dear."

"Are you sure you want to do that?" she asked as she tucked in her T-shirt and zipped her jeans.

He crossed the room and pulled her close. He brushed a kiss across her forehead, "I'm sure. I'll take care of everything. You just get ready to be Mrs. Matthew Morgan," he said.

* * * * *

"I can't believe that's the dress you wore to get married in," he said the moment they were alone in his car. They were taking their own car to the country club for lunch after the ceremony.

Because he could not get a church on such short notice, the ceremony had taken place in his parents' living room. Matthew's Uncle Thomas, a county judge, presided. Nikki Jackson, her best friend since seventh grade, had flown in from Texas to be her maid of honor. Matthew's father was their best man.

"What's wrong with my dress? It's white, it's a dress and it's classy looking. I thought I looked good in it," she said, looking down at her dress.

True it was just a sundress she bought at the end of season sale last fall, but she had only worn it twice before. It still looked fresh and new. The dress had spaghetti straps, then floated over her body to end at her calves in a handkerchief hem. She'd paid more for the new white pumps than she had for the dress, but she thought it made a good looking wedding dress on such short notice.

"Why didn't you buy a real wedding dress?" he asked.

"Because you can't go into a store and buy a wedding dress off the rack. It takes months to have a dress made, then have fittings and alterations done."

"You could have chosen something more appropriate. That thing makes you look a wide as a house from behind. Not what a bride should look like on her wedding day."

"I'm sorry," she said. Of course he was right. She should have chosen a more suitable dress.

"It's okay, honey. You're young and have great potential. We just have to work on some of your choices. Now come on, everyone's waiting," he said as he parked next to his parents' Lincoln Town Car.

* * * * *

She moved into Matthew's house during the days before the wedding. The house and its décor were a designer's dream, all sleek and shiny with lots of glass, chrome and leather. Even the pictures on the walls and knick-knacks were Matthew's designer's choices. Every time she made a suggestion or bought something, he overruled her choices. She'd once overheard him tell his father that she did not have the creative sense to decorate a doghouse.

The only room she was allowed to change was the downstairs guest bathroom. Matthew never went in that room, so he did not care how it looked. After she finished painting and decorating the room to her liking, she forced Matthew through the door with a grin and "Tadaaaa."

She hoped when he saw how beautiful this room had turned out that he would let her make a few changes in the rest of the house.

His response blew a hole in her balloon of happiness. "Well, it's interesting," he said without bothering to look closely at her hard work. He did not see the hand towels she'd embroidered or the scented soap and candles she'd ordered special for the room.

He turned and pushed past her out into the hall. "Close the door. The world doesn't need to know what the bathroom looks like. When's dinner?" He walked away without a backward glance. Not once since that day had he been in that room.

After that, he began questioning or criticizing every decision she made. From what shoes she wore to what she served for dinner to how she wore her hair. Everything she did or said or chose was wrong. Because she was so much younger than he was and from a middle class family, she assumed he knew best. After all, he had been raised in an upper class household and was nine years older and wiser. Time and again she bit her lip and gave in to his suggestions or demands for change.

Holding out or defying him garnered her snide comments or outright insults. He seemed to take great delight in pointing out her every fault in painful, elaborate detail. When he ran out of areas she needed to improve upon, he would start at the top of the list again.

The first few times he did this she responded with a few suggestions or observations of her own. Instead of listening quietly as she'd done while he talked, he would cut her off mid-sentence.

She felt she was giving an accurate assessment of his faults when he would snarl, "You really should not come into an argument unarmed. You're too easy a target."

Then he would start again on his list of insults, suggestions and demands for change. The only way to stop him was to shut up and give in, then try to figure out how to make the changes he wanted. She wondered if at times he was not correct in his assessment of her failings.

Tears were a waste of energy. They brought no sympathy or apology though they did end his rampages as he could not abide crying. With a grunt, he would grab a beer and move to his recliner to brood for the rest of the evening. The last few years he would storm out to visit his favorite bar to gain sympathy from men who agreed with his point of view.

Those were the nights she dreaded more than any others. On those nights, she would go to bed at her usual time, but in self-defense she rarely slept deeply. She would hug the edge of the mattress on her half of the queen-size bed and pray for him to pass out as soon as he slid between the sheets.

The times she did doze off, she would jerk awake at the sound of his key in the lock. She would listen as he staggered through the house to the bathroom. Once there he would fart, burp and pee. After brushing his teeth he would strip down to his silk boxers. One more burp before flipping out the bathroom light and entering the bedroom, his plan being a quick fuck as an apology.

Chapter 3

As the memories rewound, she realized there was no single incident she could point to and say, "That's the moment I stopped being strong and independent and became the spineless doormat that Matthew now walks all over."

It was not any one thing; it was a snowballing of all the little things. The cutting comments, complaints and joking putdowns that ground away at her confidence, esteem and sense of self. Like water dripping ceaselessly on a stone, Matthew had eroded away at her once fiery spirit until it was just a pile of dust sitting in her butt.

Taking a long, hard look at her life had not been fun, but it did help her. She knew she could not go on as she had. She could not continue living in the shadows of Matthew's less than stellar life. She could not remain an unpaid servant to the man she was not sure had ever really loved her. The man she had come to resent for living his life as he pleased while she sat in his two thousand square foot house and waited. She deferred to him on everything.

She made no decisions, had no opinions, except to agree with his, whether she agreed or not.

I will grow a backbone. I will do whatever I have to so I can escape and start living a life of my own.

She crawled from the bed feeling old and creaky. After washing her face and blowing her nose, she went to the kitchen and pulled the phone book out from under the phone.

It took three calls before she reached someone who could help her. Someone who could take time a few minutes to answer the questions she had.

"Let's begin with your name," the woman at the Coalition Against Family Violence said after confirming she had, finally, called the right place.

"Do you have to know my name?" she asked. Matthew seemed to know everyone in town. She did not want word of this conversation to get back to him in any way, shape or form.

"No, it's not vital. My name's Jane. What can I do for you today?"

"I want to leave my husband, but I don't know how," she whispered. "He treats me like dirt and I can't live like this any longer."

"Would you like to come into the office and talk about it?"

"Do I have to?" she asked. She did not want to risk being seen going into their offices. "Can't you just help me on the phone?"

"We don't normally do it this way, but..."

"Well, then, thanks."

"Wait, please don't hang up. Does he hit you, hurt you physically?" Jane asked.

"He's never lifted a hand to hurt me. He doesn't have to. His words do enough damage," she answered, surprised at the acid bitterness of her tone.

"Does he make fun of you, put you down, isolate you from your friends? Does he do or say things that made you feel like a child? Does he call you names and ignore your thoughts and opinions?" Jane asked in a gentle tone. "Does he demand sex whether or not you want it?"

She could not answer. Tears she thought had all been cried out swelled up again, choking her. She had to swallow twice, then clear her throat, before she could whisper, "Yes."

"Sweetie, that's called emotional or verbal abuse. Demanding sex when you don't want it is called sexual abuse. Emotional abuse is often more devastating than physical abuse. With physical abuse you can point to the scars and bruises to show the world how he hurt you. With emotional or verbal abuse, the scars are inside, on your heart, on your soul. The first step to overcoming the abuse is to make sure you're ready to leave him," Jane said gently, sounding like she spoke from personal experience.

"How do I do that?" she asked.

"There are several lists you can make that will help you look at your life with an objective eye. If you decide to leave there are things you will want to take with you and things you need to plan for."

"First make a list of his good and bad points. A kind of pro and con list. Keep in mind you need to look at your marriage for the long term, five years, ten years, even twenty years into the future. The second is a list of everything you want or need to take with you. Go through your house room by room while you make that list. Don't forget your important papers like birth and marriage certificates, insurance papers, passport. You'll also want to start an escape fund," Jane said.

She wrote as fast as she could, but was having a hard time keeping up. "Escape fund?" she asked, frowning at her notes.

"You're going to need money to start over, whether you stay in town or move somewhere else. Money for rent, furniture, utilities and a lawyer. Do you have a job?"

"No. I haven't worked in nearly ten years," she admitted. "He thought it best if I stayed home and took care of him."

"Before I left my my first husband I found a job that paid enough to live on. I started my own checking account and saved enough money for three months of living expenses. I also put my car in my name alone and got a credit card account in my name alone for emergencies."

"How do I do all that?" she asked, tears continuing to well up and overflow. There was so much she needed to do and think about and decide.

Decision-making would be the hardest part. She was out of practice. Matthew never allowed her to make even the simplest of decisions. She was now faced with life-altering choices.

"One step at a time, sweetie. There's one more list I want you to work on. I want you to write down everything you know," Jane said.

"Everything I know?" She frowned, not understanding though she jotted the list title on the page with the others.

"Yes, everything you know. You are smart; otherwise you would not be talking to me. You are strong; otherwise you would not have lasted this long in your marriage. I bet you can find a job this week and be just fine. Bank your money and make your plans without telling him, if you can. It's a short trip from verbal abuse to physical abuse, especially if he is already abusing you sexually. Remember you are a woman, one of the stronger sex. You can do anything you want. You just have to decide what it is that you want."

She had to smile. Jane had a very positive, comforting way of looking at things. "Thank you," she said, wiping at the tears that continued to stream down her cheeks.

"There is a battered women's support group meets Monday evenings at 6:30. They would be a good resource for you."

"I can't get away in the evenings," she said. "But I'll keep that in mind."

"If you want to talk again or need information or referrals, please call. We're here to help," Jane said.

"Thanks, I'll remember that."

After hanging up, she looked at her notes and filled them out with other thoughts. Rereading them, she sighed and wiped at her cheeks. She had a lot of work to do before she could leave. Matthew had their money tied up somewhere and kept all the records at his office. She only had a couple of hundred in the household checking account for food and household necessities. Matthew paid all the major bills—utilities, mortgage, etc.

She did not know how much rent on an apartment was these days or how much utilities cost. These were things she would have to find out. She had to find a job. It would have to be entry level, but until she saved up her escape fund anything would do. She would get a second job if she needed to, after she left Matthew.

She heard the familiar roar of a sportscar racing down the street and checked her watch. Was it time already? She was not ready to face him. But her watch showed that it was, indeed 5:20. Matthew was home for work. She wiped her face on a clean dishtowel she had not put away and headed for the kitchen.

"Honey, you got dinner yet? The fish are waiting!" Matthew called as he burst through the back door.

She shoved her notebook deep into her large purse. Matthew never went in there. He said he was afraid he might fall in and never find his way out again.

Thank Heavens for leftovers that were ready in two minutes in the microwave. Matthew's dinner of leftover spaghetti hit the table as he emerged from the bedroom dressed in raggedy jeans with holes in both knees and a faded T-shirt advertising a local microbrewery. Since she was not hungry, she poured herself a glass of iced tea and forced herself to sit with him while he ate. She listened without saying a word as he groused about his day, his coworkers and the state of his life in general. Not once did he ask about her day.

Twenty minutes after he breezed through the back door from work, he blew back out again. As he left, he brushed a kiss across her cheek. "See you Sunday afternoon. I should be home in time for dinner," he said, pulling the door shut behind him.

She went to the front window and watched as he drove past. Once the roar of his car's powerful engine died away, she dug the notebook out of her purse. Moving from room to room, she followed Jane's instructions and made a list of everything she wanted to take with her. It took less than an hour to go through the entire house. It was a pitifully short list.

Matthew's choices were not hers. All she wanted were her clothes, the half dozen pairs of brass candlesticks she had collected and two quilts.

Her grandmother had given her one of the quilts when she graduated from high school. The second was the quilt she and her mother had made together the summer she turned twelve. She had learned the basics of sewing while making that crazy quilt. The quilts had been stored in the guestroom closet just after their wedding. It was either pack them away or Matthew would donate them to Goodwill. He refused to have them on display anywhere in HIS house.

Saturday morning she took on her closet. She pulled every piece of clothing out and made two piles. The clothes she wore, liked and felt comfortable wearing—her choice of clothing—were piled on the bed. The other clothes, the clothes Matthew had chosen, were tossed to the floor. That pile contained the short-short skirts and clingy see-through tops that a mature teenager would not wear. Most of them had not fit since she gained twenty pounds five years before.

One of Matthew's biggest points of contention was her weight. She did not like the extra pounds either, but as an emotional eater, she had hard time sticking with a diet or exercise program with any dedication when she felt as depressed as she had the last few years.

Once she sorted and thinned out the clothes, she stuffed the ones on the floor into three large black garbage bags. She also packed up a box of romance novels she had finished reading. She piled everything in the back seat of her car and drove to the thrift shop that supported the local women's shelter. With the help of a volunteer, she unloaded and felt ten pounds lighter. She would never miss those clothes, though she wasn't sure how Matthew would feel the next time he went through her closet to choose an outfit for whatever social engagement he demanded she attend with him. To her knowledge that would not be until

Christmas when company policy and his father demanded she attend the office Christmas dinner.

She wandered the store for a few minutes to see what was offered for sale. After strolling up and down every aisle, she stopped and studied a rack offering information pamphlets. She took several that dealt with abuse, how to recognize it and how to escape.

She returned home after running a few other errands she'd been putting off. After fixing a cup of tea, she took out her notebook to work on the other lists Jane had given her. "Make a list of what you know..."

So what do I know about myself?

I am smart. I am funny. I can sing, dance and play softball. I am in good health. I am a hard worker. I can learn anything I want to. I am young enough to change. I am stronger than I think. I can make it on my own.

Each entry took longer than the one before to thin up. Each entry was written with less and less confidence than the one before it. She was not sure about anything anymore. She was especially uncertain if she could make it on her own after leaving Matthew.

Sunday morning she looked over her notes again and added to them where she could. "So what now?" she asked herself aloud. "Now you will find a job and start your escape fund," she answered herself in the same bewildered tone.

She had been talking aloud to herself for as long as she could remember. She was the one person who always paid attention to what she had to say. Her thoughts seemed to become more tangible after she said them aloud, even if only to herself. Someone once told her that talking to herself was okay. Answering herself was fine, too, as long as she did not answer in a different voice. So she talked to herself when she needed to hear the arguments aloud in order to make the best decision.

Matthew questioned her talking aloud from time to time, but lately he never heard anything she said whether she was talking to herself or to him. She could be in the middle of telling him about something that was important to her and he would change the subject and never give her a chance to finish what she was trying to say.

Picking up the classified ad section of the New Bern Sun Journal, she flipped to the help wanted pages. She read each entry, but she was not qualified to be a trucker, did not have a nursing or sales background and had no desire to be a garbage-person for the city, no matter how much the job paid. She was about to give up when she reached the last entry.

URGENTLY NEEDED: Organized person to run two-man office. Computer and phone skills required. Bilingual preferred, but not required. Apply in person

C&JJ Bail Bonds

She read the ad a second, then a third time. She had enough computer knowledge to surf the Internet, type and print letters and even put together an occasional spreadsheet or report for Matthew. She could talk on the phone, though Matthew often criticized her for being abrupt with people. He never understood he had trained her to get her thoughts across in ten seconds or less. She had learned to speak in sound bites. She could be friendly and expansive. She could be business-like or casual. She could be anything they wanted as long as they gave her the job.

The only thing that might hold her back was the bilingual part. She would offer to take conversational Spanish classes at the community college if they wanted. She would learn to stand on her head and juggle oranges if they asked her to. Whatever it took for them to hire her and paid her a decent wage.

"Okay, so maybe you found a job. How are you going to tell Matthew you're going to work?" she asked herself aloud.

"Maybe you won't have to," her logical side answered silently.

* * * * *

After she finished all the lists Jane has suggested, she felt the urge to talk her plans over with someone who would not go running to Matthew with the news. The list of such confidants was a short one. Her parents would not discuss divorce with her, her sister would not care, so she called Nikki.

She and Nikki had been best friends since the first day of seventh grade when Nikki settled into the chair next to her in the lunchroom and began talking about how cute the boys had grown over the summer. She had agreed and their friendship had grown from there. In the years since, they had gotten into and out of trouble together, shared good times and heartaches alike and stood as witness when the other married.

It was late that afternoon when she finally reached Nikki. After initial greetings and catching up on the three months since their last conversation, she made the announcement. "I'm thinking of leaving Matthew. I can't live like this any more."

"So why are you still there? You should have left the son of a bitch six months after the wedding," Nikki said, her tone sharp. "You've been unhappy for years. Why don't you just kick his sorry ass to the street and take everything?"

"I haven't decided anything yet. I just know I cannot go on like this," she whispered.

Nikki remained silent.

"Problem is, I don't know how to do this. How do I leave the man I vowed to spend the rest of my life with? The man I've given up the last ten years of my life for?" She wiped away her tears as she paced through the house, kitchen to dining room to living room then back into the kitchen again.

"The troll vowed to love, cherish and protect you. He broke his vows first when he crushed your spirit. All you're doing by getting out is saving yourself before he can do any more damage."

"Yes, but..." she tried to argue, only did not have a winning argument in her.

"You need to do OBTAD," Nikki advised sounding confident.

"What are you talking about? Obtad?"

"Years ago my mother dragged me to this therapist to help me overcome my shyness and lack of self esteem."

"You? Shy and lacking self-esteem? I don't believe it," she snorted. Nikki was one of the boldest, most outgoing, self-assured women she knew. She wanted to grow up to be just like her.

"I was such a shy child I could not look anyone in the eye. I talked to people's shoes and pets. That therapist told me about OBTAD. Once I started practicing it my confidence and self esteem grew and I became the woman you're talking to today. Do I sound like an infomercial or what?"

"So, what is OBTAD?"

"One Brave Thing A Day. Once a day you have to step out of your comfort zone and do something brave, something you would not normally do. Whether it's making a phone call to someone about something or going out and buying an outfit you normally would not dare to buy or stand up to your husband and tell him off. All it takes is one tiny step and you'll be amazed at how good you feel. Soon you'll be moving beyond just one thing a day. Some days you might even be able to do two or three things that are brave."

She listened as Nikki continued to lecture on doing brave things. It was simple, so simple. All it took was doing one small, new, brave thing. She could do one small thing. If not every day, at least two or three times a week. It wouldn't take long before she was as brave and bold as her friend was, she hoped.

"OBTAD," she murmured.

"OBTAD," Nikki echoed. "You can do this. I know you can."

"I'll try," she said.

"E-mail me every day. Tell me what your brave thing is and how it turned out. It helps to have to account to someone about your OBTAD."

Before she could agree, the kitchen door opened. She jerked and said, "I've got to go."

"Mr. Troll come home?" Nikki snarled.

"Yes. I'll talk to you soon."

"Keep me informed. You know you're always welcome to move here..."

"I know. Talk to you soon."

Before Nikki could say anything further, she hung up, hoping Matthew had not noticed. As usual, luck was not to be hers.

"Who was on the phone? You sounded awfully chummy." Matthew asked as he entered the kitchen and dropped his bag on the floor. He walked away as she answered, knowing she would follow him through the house.

"Nikki."

"Oh, her. What did the wicked bitch of the West have to say?"

"Not much, we were just catching up. It had been a while since we'd last talked."

"I don't know what you two have to talk about anyway. She's a man-hating business shark who lives her life in bars and you're a house frau who hides from life," Matthew grumbled as he pulled off his dirty, T-shirt that reeked of fish and beer and sweat.

"She's my friend. You don't have to understand it," she said, a coating of strength returning to her spine. Picking up the clothes he dropped on the bedroom floor on his way to the shower, she retreated to the kitchen. After putting the clothes in the washing machine, she started dinner

After his shower, Matthew settled into his leather recliner with the Sunday paper and a beer. He did not move until she called him to dinner. After inhaling the meal of soup and sandwiches, he returned to the living room to watch the Weather Channel, then an old war movie while she cleaned the kitchen.

While her hands were washing dishes, her mind drifted. *I need a plan, a-step-by-step-guide. Why isn't there such a thing?*

Something called "The Emotional Cripple's Guide to Leaving an Abusive SOB" would be most helpful. Only such a book did not exist, at least she did not think it did. She would have to check on the Internet tomorrow. Once she left Matthew and rebuilt her life, maybe she would write just such a book. It would be an instant best seller if she sent a copy to Oprah or Dr. Phil to share with other emotionally abused and crippled women.

For now she would worry about getting a job and doing one brave thing each day to set her plan on leaving into motion.

You can do this. All it takes is faith, courage and one brave thing a day.

Chapter 4

At 9:20 that evening, Matthew pushed out of his chair and stretched with a long, loud groan. "It's been a hell of a weekend. I'm beat. I'm going to bed. You coming?"

She looked at him, forcing herself to keep her expression neutral. "Not yet. I want to watch this movie." The last thing she wanted was to go to bed in the middle of this movie.

She had waited for more than a month since the first commercials began touting this romantic comedy was coming to television. She'd wanted to see it since it was in the theaters last year. Matthew never took her to the movies. He preferred to rent DVDs so he could stop and start and back up whenever he wanted. Problem was that he liked action/adventure shoot 'em up gunfights and she preferred dramas and romantic comedies. Which meant they watched a lot of action/adventure movies. Only occasionally did she win on selecting their once a week movie rental—usually when the film was based on a true story.

"All right, good night," he said, crossing the room and smacking a kiss across the air just above her lips.

She did not protest. Why bother? If she did, he would only demand she come to bed so he could kiss her properly. Right now for some reason she would rather punch him in the nose than debate his kiss quality. Two and a half days of stewing in her own juices and thinking about the past ten years had filled her gut with an acid that still burned like a forest fire.

But she could not, would not do anything about it yet. She had plans to make, a job to secure and an escape to set in place. Tipping her hand at this point would not get her out of this farce of a marriage. It would only cause her more pain as he ground her further under his shoe heels.

She followed the movie's dialogue with only one ear. The other was listening to Matthew as he went through his nightly routine of preparing for bed. She checked the clock when the bed finally creaked and silence descended over the back of the house.

Ten minutes later, during a commercial break, she rose from the corner of the couch that she'd claimed as her own. Crossing the living room, she stopped just out of sight of the bedroom. She stood and listened. It took a moment to block the television and the sounds of her own heartbeat and breathing, but finally she heard it. Matthew snuffling in his sleep. In a couple minutes the snoring would begin.

He was asleep, out for the night. A weekend of beer and fresh air had knocked him flat. She could invite a brass band to rehearse in the living room and he would not wake up. He would not rouse until his alarm went beep-beep-beep at 6:18. Until then he would not know or care if she were in the bed next to him or out driving around town.

Taking a deep breath, she worked to relax the muscles across her shoulders and up the back of her neck. It took a few minutes, but they finally eased. Her shoulders no longer felt like they were brushing against her earlobes.

Going to her purse in the kitchen, she pulled out her notebook and a pen. Then she retrieved the classified ads section from the jumbled pile of discarded Sunday newspaper by Matthew's chair.

She returned to her seat and opened the paper. After re-reading the ad from C&JJ Bail Bonds for the twentieth time that day, she copied the ad word for word into her notebook on the back of the page where she had drafted her pitifully scanty resume.

What am I doing? Am I really going to try and get this job? What if I get it? How long will I be able to keep it before Matthew finds out and makes me quit or gets me fired?

For the next hour and a half that the movie ran, she forced herself to pay attention to what was happening on the television screen and not worry with what might or might not happen the next morning. Once the eleven o'clock news began, she flipped her notebook open and read through the pages of notes and thoughts and lists she had compiled over the weekend. Once she read through everything, she realized that, except for money to leave, she was well on her way out the door. She knew she wanted her freedom, she just had to figure out how to pay for it.

Turning to a fresh page, she wrote "$5000.00" in the top margin. It was a random amount of money, but she would need at least that much to rent an apartment, set up housekeeping, get some basic furniture and retain an attorney. Now all she had to do was figure out how to get the money together without Matthew finding out what she was doing or why.

Yawning, she closed the notebook and returned it to the bottom of her purse. She cleaned up the pile of newspapers beside Matthew's chair and carried their empty iced tea glasses to the kitchen. After putting the dishes in the dishwasher, she tossed the newspapers into the recycle bin then locked up the house and turned out the lights.

Matthew did not shift when she climbed into bed next to him and curled up on her side facing away from him. Nor did the rhythmic snoring he always subjected her to after a weekend drinking and fishing change. She lay there for a moment listening, then rolled over to face him.

Nudging his shoulder, she said, "Matthew, roll over. The neighbors are complaining about your snoring again."

He did not respond so she put her hand on the shoulder closest to her and shook harder. "Roll over," she ordered in a louder, sterner voice.

This time he rolled away from her. The snoring stopped. She settled back down, hugging her side of the queen-size bed and stared at the wall. There was a good two feet of empty bed between their backs. That space would remain between them throughout the night, a symbol of the chasm that had grown in their marriage over the last ten years.

She lay next to her husband for a long time hoping, dreaming, praying that things went the way she planned and she could find her way out of the emptiness her life had become.

* * * * *

"Shit, I'm late." Matthew's muttered curse and the elbow he jabbed in the middle of her back woke her the next morning. She jerked awake then stared at the watch on her left wrist through bleary eyes. She had not fallen asleep until long after midnight and then every hour she woke to stare at the clock across the room. She finally fell asleep just before daybreak. Now, less than an hour later, Matthew was demanding she panic with him.

"Didn't you set your alarm?" she asked as she sat up and threw back the comforter. Reaching to the floor she grabbed the sweatpants she wore under her oversized sleep-shirt.

"I guess I forgot. Fix me some coffee, okay?"

"Uh huh," she said, as she stood and stretched. Her heart still raced from the rude awakening, but she refused to panic just because they'd overslept. Though Matthew was supposed to be at work at eight, no one would say anything if her were late. He was a low-level executive in his father's company so no one ever said anything, no matter what Matthew did.

By the time he'd had pulled on khaki trousers, a freshly pressed white dress shirt and brown striped tie, she had zapped a cup of water in the microwave. After stirring in a rounded teaspoon of instant coffee, a teaspoon and a half of sugar and two dollops of milk, she poured the light brown coffee into the stainless steel travel cup he took to work each day. She was screwing on the lid when he flew into the kitchen.

He stopped long enough to take a sip and savor it. "I don't know how you do it. You don't drink coffee, but you make it so much better than I do."

"Just lucky I guess," she said turning to the sink to rinse out the mug she had mixed the coffee in.

"Okay, well, I'll see you for dinner. Spaghetti tonight, right?"

"Uh huh."

She did not take a relaxed breath until his car roared by the front windows. Then she turned her attention to preparing herself for her first job interview in more than ten years.

After going through her closet and deciding on a pair of stone gray slacks and a deep red imitation silk blouse, she headed for the shower. Needing a shot of confidence, she decided to take what Nikki called a "girly shower." She shaved carefully and used her favorite shower gel and super duper conditioner. She stayed in the hot shower until the water ran cold. Only then did she climb out, dry off and apply lotion to her entire body. After dressing, she blew her hair dry and spent a few minutes putting on the makeup she hardly ever wore. After slipping on a pair of black loafers, she was ready to go and secure the job that was give her freedom.

She spent a few minutes making the bed and cleaning up the bedroom. She put a load of clothes in the washing machine. In her orderly life, Mondays was laundry day. She did not want Matthew to fuss because his Tuesday pair of boxers was still in the laundry hamper and not clean and folded in his dresser like they were supposed to be.

After grabbing a Pepsi from the crisper drawer in the refrigerator, she headed out. She drove through the Post Office parking lot to drop off the bills Matthew had left for her to mail.

Then she went to Burger King for a bacon, egg and cheese croissant. Then she headed downtown, eating breakfast as she drove. She drove to the courthouse then turned left onto Craven Street. As soon as she passed the big brick courthouse and its parking lot across the street, she began checking houses for street numbers while at the same time looking for an open parking space.

She slowed as she passed 422 Craven Street. This wasn't an office building. This was a house. A historic home that, if she could remember correctly, had been empty for about ten years. From the debris and building supplies on the front porch it looked like someone was renovating. Were they building offices? Or was the bail bond business a back room, home-based enterprise?

She jumped when a big blue truck pulled up close behind her and honked, a long, loud sound that echoed up and down the street. With her face burning, she sped up and circled the block again. This time around she came to a full stop in front of the building. There was a dirt and gravel driveway between this house and the one next door. There was a piece of cardboard taped to the front window, but she could not read what was written on it.

A movement in her rearview mirror had her glancing up. The blue truck was back. She rounded the block one more time. This time she turned into the driveway instead of just driving past it. She followed the dirt and gravel track around behind the house. The entire back yard had been turned into a parking lot. She pulled into the space as far from the house as she could get.

Climbing from the car, she walked down the driveway to the front porch. It was 9:20, but the front door was locked. She knocked, but no one answered. The piece of cardboard in the window had C&JJ Bail Bonds written on it, but there were no office hours posted. The porch was filled the piles building debris, stacks of lumbar and other building supplies. There was nowhere to sit so she walked back down the driveway and returned to her car. She opened her windows a couple of inches, locked the doors and settled in to wait for someone to show up.

After five minutes she was bored. She had nothing to read and did not want to work on her lists any more. It now depressed her to see all the things she needed to finish before she left. Adjusting her seat back a couple of notches to a more comfortable position, she closed her eyes and listened to the sounds of the neighborhood. In a few minutes she had relaxed into a state somewhere between sleep and consciousness.

Chapter 5

She was in Matthew's office dressed in a designer suit and high heeled pumps, two things she never wore. She stood in front of his desk offering him a fist full of hundred dollar bills. The hitch was he had to sign the divorce decree in her other hand. She was not sure where the stack of money she was offering came from, but somehow she was rich, rich, rich.

At first he stared at her in shock before asking, "Where did you get that kind of money? You're not good for anything."

She leaned over his desk and handed him a Montblanc pen. "Since you think I'm so worthless then you won't mind signing this. Then you'll be free to look for a woman who is everything you think I'm not."

He had just put pen to paper when a screech of brakes, male cursing and a slamming car door invaded her dream. She jerked awake for the second time that morning and found herself sleeping in her car. Glancing at her watch she was surprised to find it was 10:55. She had drifted in and out of sleep for almost an hour and a half.

Blinking and trying to clear the fog from her brain, she turned when knuckles thumped against the driver's glass. She rolled the window down a few more inches after making sure the door was locked. "May I help you?" she asked in as professional a voice as she could manage.

She looked up and lost her train of thought. The man peering in the window had the most intriguing face she'd ever seen. Even bruised, bloody and streaked with dirt and sweat, he was beautiful. She was tempted to take up sketching, painting or sculpting just so she could capture the bold lines and planes that made up his face. Too bad she had no artistic talent.

"Who the hell are you and what are you doing in my space?" he demanded, his voice a deep and dark growl.

"I'm sorry. I didn't see a sign reserving this space. If you'll tell me where to park, I'll be happy to move," she said, hoping to keep the peace.

"Don't worry about it. What do you want?" he blinked and his entire demeanor softened. It was as if he had reminded himself that she could be a potential client. That is, if he were a part of C&JJ Bail Bonds.

"O-B-T-A-D," she reminded herself. She unlocked the door and reached for the handle. "I'm here about the job advertised in yesterday's newspaper. Are you C or JJ?" she asked, slowly pushing the door open, hoping he would move out of the way.

He straightened and backed up two steps, but did not say anything. He just looked her up and down.

"Could we go inside and discuss this? Or are job interviews always held in the parking lot?" she asked.

Now that he'd straightened and she was standing without the security of a car door between them, a chill of nerves skittered up her back. She had never considered herself a small woman, especially since gaining weight, but standing before this man she felt petite. He was at least a foot taller than her five feet four and looked like a walking wall. Broad shoulders and chest layered with muscles bulged under a long-sleeved, black, three-button

Henley. Narrow waist and hips segued into long legs clothed in black camouflage pants and hiking boots.

"Wow," she murmured under her breath.

"Cody? What's going on?" Another man approached slowly. He, too, was dressed in black. Though he was several inches shorter than the man he had addressed as Cody was, he was even broader and more muscular. His skin was the color of espresso, but his deep brown eyes were the gentlest she had ever seen. They reminded her of Lady, the cocker-terrier mutt she'd owned as a child. He stared at her, his curious expression sliding away until he appeared as dangerous as a hungry panther.

"It's okay, JJ. She's here about the job," the man before her said.

"Oh, thank God. Take her inside and put her to work," JJ said. He turned away and began unloading the back of the black Tahoe parked next to her sedan.

"I've got to get to the courthouse. You interview her," Cody growled. He moved like he was in pain as he stalked across the small parking lot.

"Are you all right?" she asked as she followed him.

"I'm exhausted, mad as hell and late for court. Excuse me," he said. He pushed through the blueberry blue door and disappeared.

She remained where she was, uncertain. *Is this really where I want to work? How do I get the job when no one will talk to me? What am I doing here?*

"Could you get the door?" the man called JJ asked.

She nodded as she stepped out of his way. As powerfully built as he was he struggled under the weight of the two dufflebags hanging from his shoulders. In one hand he balanced a tray of half-empty coffee cups. The other held a plastic grocery bag overflowing with trash.

"Do you need some help?" she asked, pulling the door open wide.

"Thanks, but I've got it. Go on up front to the office. I'll be there as soon as I dump this stuff," he smiled warmly as he passed her.

She followed him into the building, pulling the door closed behind her. Then she paused to allow her eyes to adjust to the dim interior. After a few seconds, her eyes widened at the state of chaos the hallway was in.

She picked her way around the stepladders, piles of paint cans and tarps that filled the hall. The walls were yellowed with age. One wall had an open hole in it exposing old copper pipes that ran vertically inside the wall. Light came into the hall from several open doorways along the hall. Looking up, she noted a single exposed bulb attached to the ceiling with no globe covering it.

As she passed the open doorways, curiosity got the best of her. She peeked in each of the rooms as she passed. What had once been the kitchen had been stripped of all appliances, leaving only the built-in cabinetry in place. The room had once been white, but time had turned it a dingy gray from age, grease and neglect. The next room was empty, other than a card table, two folding chairs and a county map that had been duct-taped to the old turquoise paint on the wall.

She reached a king-size flowered sheet hanging from the ceiling. Pulling one side of the sheet away from the wall, she stepped through. On this side of the curtain the hall was painted a soft yellow and the restored hardwood floors were covered with a large Oriental rug. To her left was a conference room. The walls had been painted a soothing peach color, the floors refinished, furniture and accessories in place. A long oak table with six chairs filled this room. One wall held a number of frames containing what looked like licenses, awards and certificates of achievement. Other frames highlighted newspaper clippings. She was tempted to step closer so she could examine these, but that would have to wait. She would snoop later, after she won the job.

She turned to the other room, got as far as the doorway and froze. Here was the heart and soul of C&JJ Bail Bonds. A pair of desks had been pushed together in the middle of the room. Five gunmetal gray filing cabinets stood at attention along the back wall, flanking a door that led toward other rooms at the back of the house. She now understood why JJ wanted to put her to work at once.

Both desks, all four chairs and the top of all the filing cabinets were piled high with papers. She thought she saw a computer on one of the desks, but who could tell for sure?

"It looks like you've had an explosion," she said, hoping her observation came across as witty, not critical.

"You could say that. The last girl didn't know crap about organization. When we fired her, this was what the room looked like. We've been so busy we haven't had time to do much more than add to it."

"How long was she here?" she asked out of morbid curiosity.

"A week. She's been gone for two. The temp agencies refuse to send us any more replacements. They say we're too demanding." JJ began moving stacks of papers from chair to one of the desks. He swore under his breath when the towering pile slid away from him. Half the files landed on the floor at his feet, creating an even bigger mess.

"Please, have a seat," he said, waving her toward the now empty chair.

As soon as she was seated, he disappeared back out into the hall. She heard him run up the stairs. After a few minutes of silence, she pulled the stack of files sitting in the middle of the desk closer. She never realized a bail bond service had so much paperwork, or so many clients. She examined the top few files, noting each had a year, name and a four-digit code to identify them.

Hoping her actions might influence the two men, she began to sort the files by year. When she finished the first pile, she reached for another stack and continued. She separated loose papers and unopened mail into other piles. Once she'd sorted the files by year, she began sorting each year into alphabetical order.

"What the hell do you think you're doing?" Cody growled from the doorway, startling her.

Okay, so maybe she had overstepped the bounds, but Matthew had trained her well. Any mess on the order of this office would give her nightmares for weeks, whether or not she got the job. She had to do something to help put order to this disaster area.

"You need help and I need a job. I figured if I gave a small demonstration of my filing skills you might be more amenable to hiring me," she responded without looking in his direction or stopping her hands from what they were doing.

"You won't last a week. You're too..." he paused.

"Too what?" she asked. Turning in her chair, she looked the man in the eye for about four seconds before turning back to the files in her lap. Such pretty caramel brown eyes that seemed to see the quivering mass of jelly that was hiding just under her skin. His lashes were too long and too thick for a man. On him, though, with his sharply angled face, they made him appear even more masculine.

"Too pretty, too neat, too classy, too society," Cody answered.

She sat stunned for a moment and then began to laugh. He thought she was too classy. With hair she trimmed herself twice a year and clothes bought from a discount catalog's end of season sale he thought she was too society. When she realized he was staring at her like she had grown a second head, she forced herself to get serious. He did not know anything about her except what he saw.

"Let me assure you I am anything but classy and society. I want this job. I NEED this job. I have to have it." Her tone grew more desperate with each sentence, but she did not care.

If she had to get down on her knees and kiss the dust covered Oriental rug in the hall, she would. She would do whatever she had to for this job. She had no pride left to be picky. Matthew had crumbled that along with her backbone years ago. She had nothing left to lose. If she did not get this job she would be forced to stay with Matthew forever.

At that moment, JJ appeared in the hallway. She was certain he could read fear in her eyes, though she was focused on the papers in her lap. "Aren't you late for court?" he asked his partner.

Cody swore softly and grabbed the briefcase sitting by the front door. "Yeah, I'm late. Explain to this lady why she won't work out, okay?"

"I'll take care of it," JJ said with a smirk.

As soon as the door slammed shut behind his partner, JJ yawned and turned to face her. "You're hired for a thirty-day trial. When can you start?"

She looked at the man, eyes wide and feeling like she'd fallen down the rabbit hole with Alice. "Excuse me?"

"You're hired. We need someone nine to three on weekdays. The office is closed weekends and anytime the courthouse is closed," JJ said. "Oh, yeah. The job pays ten dollars an hour. When can you start?"

Her eyes widened at the mention of holidays and salary. She looked out the window at Cody striding toward the courthouse. "I guess I started five minutes ago," she said. "Could you tell me a little about the job? Like what I am supposed to be doing?"

"You run the office. Answer phones, do paperwork and filing, keep track of court dates and our schedules. If you're interested, we could even train you to be a bail enforcement agent."

"What's a bail enforcement agent?" she asked.

"The politically correct term for bounty hunter. They're also known as bond or bail enforcement agents. We pay the bond for our clients who get themselves arrested. Bond guarantees they will show up for their court dates. If they don't show, we have to track them down and return them to jail or we lose the money we put up. Cody and I do most of our own bail enforcement. Sometimes when things get boring around here, we'll even track for the sheriff's department."

"Sounds dangerous," she said when he finished his lecture. *And exciting*.

"Rarely dangerous. Most of our clients are nonviolent. DWIs, bad checks, petty theft. Not a lot of money involved in any one case, but as you can see, lots of paperwork." JJ said before yawning again.

"Yeah, well, okay. I'm going to figure out the filing system so I can try to get this mess under control. You go sleep," she said.

JJ nodded then turned and clomped back up the stairs. She listened as he walked around the second floor. She heard water running in what she assumed was a shower, more walking, a series of squeaks and squawks and then silence.

When she finished collecting and sorting all the piles of paper in the room, her stomach growled and cramped in protest. She looked at her watch and was shocked to see it was almost two o'clock. She called her favorite Chinese restaurant and placed an order for delivery. When her lunch arrived, she carried the pint of fried rice out onto the front porch and ate sitting on the steps. Once she'd settled the gnawing hunger, she returned to the office and her new job.

By the time she finished sorting all the files from the loose paperwork, it was ten minutes to four. Taking a blank note card out, she marked down her hours and the half-hour she took for lunch. Then she put the card in the top drawer of the desk she had claimed for her own. With a tired, contented sigh and a wistful smile, she left her new job.

* * * * *

Sad brown eyes haunted Cody though he tried to avoid thinking about them or their owner. Those eyes held deep secrets he would rather not learn about. He needed a human pit bull who would not take crap from anyone—him included.

But those brown eyes. His sister had had that same expression in her eyes, that same sad aura about her. Only with Shelly he had not recognized it for what it was, signs of deep, serious problems that she did not share with anyone. It was not until she had committed suicide that he realized the husband who had always been so friendly, outgoing and personable, was actually an abusive SOB who had sent his wife into such a deep depression she killed herself to escape him and their marriage.

By the time Cody left the courthouse at the end of the day, he was not sure what he could do for the sad woman, but knew he had to do something. Guilt still ate at his heart and his gut for not stepping into Shelly's private business before it was too late.

Though he was certain she would never work out, maybe working a week or two could ease some of her sadness. That would also give them time to find someone more appropriate for the job. Someone less fragile. Someone more street savvy.

JJ was just coming down the stairs when Cody entered the front door of the house. Though exhaustion lay on his head like ten wet blankets, he had to deal with this acidy feeling of guilt.

"How'd we do?" JJ asked when Cody handed him the briefcase.

"A husband and wife pair for passing bad checks and a DUI," Cody replied. "About that lady who was here this morning..."

"Yes?" his business partner asked, cocking one eyebrow.

"Hire her, at least on a trial basis." Cody yawned as he headed for the stairs. "She will never work out, but at least she can answer the phone until we find someone who will."

"I already did," JJ said, trying unsuccessfully to hold back a grin.

"What?" Cody stopped mid step and turned to stare at the other man.

"I already hired her for a thirty-day trial. She looks competent, intelligent and we need somebody. Something about her reminds me of Shelly. Besides, you said I could hire and fire anyone I wanted as long as you didn't have to deal with them, remember?"

"Yeah, okay, whatever," Cody growled, feeling off balance and outmaneuvered. "I'm going to bed."

"Sleep well and long enough to help your disposition." JJ called after the man who was like a brother to him. Then he turned to the kitchen, still muttering to himself. "Anyway, my mama and her sisters would skin me alive if I didn't help a woman in need. And she seemed like one needy woman."

* * * * *

She wanted to dance, sing and scream to the heavens about her new job. But she did not. She could not. Matthew could not find out about her job or he would find a way to ruin it for her. Or he would spend her money before she earned the first paycheck. He had been talking about a new fishing boat and if he knew about her job, he would buy the boat, then expect her to pay for it.

She finished the laundry as soon as she came home. By 5 o'clock she had finished putting the clean clothes away and had the Monday spaghetti with meat sauce on the stove. Her mind was not on the cooking. She was trying to figure out how long it would take her to earn the $5000 she needed to start life on her own.

It was hard to sit and eat dinner with the excitement of her new job, but somehow she managed. She waited until he had settled in for the evening with his beer and channel-changer. Then she took the portable phone to the guestroom and closed the door until the knob clicked into place. Then she dialed Nikki's cell number.

"Hey, you've reached the machine. You know what to do so do it after the beep," the recorded message played after the second ring.

"Hi Nikki, it's me. I just wanted to let you know I got a job today. Pays ten dollars an hour and they're willing to let me work six hours a day so Matthew won't need to know about it. Hopefully I'll save up enough to leave soon. Talk to you later," she said quickly before hanging up.

Her secret was no longer a secret. A secret only worked when only one person knew it. Once two people shared the secret it was bound to get out. But she felt confident that Nikki would not be calling Matthew. Her secret was safe for the moment.

* * * * *

The next morning she dressed in a long denim skirt and bright red T-shirt. As she slipped on a pair of loafers, she sent up a prayer that the job would still be hers today. After all, JJ had hired her after Cody had told her she could not have the job. She didn't want to cause a rift between the partners. Somehow, she had to change Cody's mind today. She planned to finish cleaning the office to prove herself indispensable to the C&JJ Bail Bonds operation.

By noon she finished sorting and filing the loose paperwork she had collected from around the room. Until someone showed her what the computer was used for, she was done for the day.

But the office was still a mess. Since she had a couple of hours, cleaning was the next order of business. It was nearly three when she turned on the vacuum and began to guide it around the office floor.

She was finishing up when she heard boots clomping overhead. The sound was a staccato counterpoint to the vacuum's roar. At the same time, the front door opened and someone came into the front hall. She ignored her spectators as she finished vacuuming the conference room floor.

Out of the corner of her eye, she saw JJ dressed in a black suit with a white shirt and grape jelly colored tie. Cody was pulling on a long sleeved blue chambray shirt over a black undershirt. She ignored them as she wound up the electrical cord and guided the vacuum back into the closet where she had found it. Only then did she look at the two men.

JJ looked at Cody. Cody looked at JJ. Then they both turned to stare at her.

"You did all this in one day?" Cody asked, looking around the office at the transformation.

The paperwork was gone. The room gleamed. The desktops shone. The hardwood floor reflected light. Even the windows sparkled.

"Two days, actually. I had something to prove." She turned and reached for her purse. "Messages are on the desk next to the mail. I'd appreciate someone showing me the computer programs you're using tomorrow. See you in the morning."

She left before either man could say a word. It was late and she had a chicken and rice dinner to get in the oven in the next twenty minutes. It was one of Matthew's favorite meals and it had to cook for two hours. Dinner was at half past five each and every night, no excuses, no matter what.

Once dinner was in the oven, she vacuumed, then cleaned the bathroom. She had just enough time to do a quick dusting before Matthew banged in the back door.

After dinner, she felt exhausted, but certain that she would be able to keep her job a secret. She just needed to get a little better organized and spread her cleaning chores over the week. With only the two of them, the house did not get dirty, so she would be able to clean once a week instead of every other day as she had done for the past ten years. Matthew would never notice the difference anyway.

Chapter 6

Over the next week, life settled into a busy and fulfilling routine. She mastered the office computer system with only a few minor glitches. At home, she reworked her schedule, spreading her housekeeping chores over five days. Dinners were set in stone, so all she had to do was find time for grocery shopping. With the challenge of her new job, she found herself happier than she had been in more years than she could remember. She even began humming again, a childhood habit that Matthew had broken her of shortly after their wedding.

On Sunday, Matthew's parents arrived unannounced just as she was looking in the refrigerator for something to fix for lunch. After warm greetings all around, Matthew looked at her critically. "Go change your clothes. We're hungry," he stated.

She looked down at her clothes then at him. They were both dressed in faded jeans and T-shirts. She had left her T-shirt untucked to try and camouflage the extra pounds around her middle while his was tucked in. He was even wearing a belt.

Though his shirt had several stains across the front, he meant to wear it out to eat. Hers was a size too big, but stain free. His parents had come from church, so she decided that changing might be a good thing. Especially if it kept Matthew from spending the afternoon slamming her with constructively critical complements. She had never understood how he could say things that cut her to ribbons while sounding to those around them like he loved her very much.

Without a word she slipped from the living room. She spent three minutes changing into navy slacks and a cream colored polo and another three minutes was spent running a comb through her hair and applying the minimal amount of make up that Matthew approved of.

When she returned to the living room, Matthew interrupted his mother's story of his brother's latest triumph to say, "Well it's about time. I'm starving."

"Sorry," she said, dropping her chin so his parents would not see the hurt in her eyes.

"So, let's go already," Matthew said, heading to the front door.

She followed his parents out, making sure the house was locked and she had keys and her wallet in her purse. Matthew had, on more than one occasion, taken her out to dinner only to discover he had forgotten his wallet. Glancing at his back pockets, She noted that today was yet another one of those days.

At the steakhouse his parents frequented, which had a pay-first, eat-later policy, Matthew discovered his empty pockets. He refused to allow his father to buy lunch, instead turning to her. "You have money, don't you?"

"Yes," she said, pulling out her own wallet.

"Good, pay for all four of us, okay?" With that he shooed his parents ahead of him and headed for a table across the room.

Lunch buffet and iced tea for four ate up the fifty dollars in her wallet, the entire amount she had set aside out of the monthly household budget to open her own bank account. But she only used her credit card in emergencies. When the bill came each month, Matthew demanded a penny by penny accounting of every charge. She found life easier when she paid with cash.

Her gut churning, she joined the table just as the others stood and headed for the buffet. She followed slower, fixing herself a salad and avoiding the rest. She picked at the salad, eating about half before her stomach threatened to send everything back up again.

Matthew ate his first plate of food quickly, talking to his father between bites. On returning from his second trip through the buffet he sat down, looked at her and said, "What's up with you?"

"What?" she asked, stabbing a single baby corncob and eating it.

"You're not eating, you've started humming again and you've been preoccupied a lot lately. You got a new boyfriend or something?" he asked the question in a loud accusatory tone. Not only did his parents gape at her, conversations ceased at the tables around them and all heads swung their way.

She felt her face burn as she glanced past him to the older couple at the table just over his left shoulder. They, too, were staring at her, the woman with wide-eyed horror and the man with curiosity.

Her gaze cut back to Matthew and she frowned, though her cheeks were burning at the same time. "Of course not. How can you ask such a thing?"

Matthew frowned back while cutting the piece of steak that filled the plate. "Something's different with you and I don't like it. If you don't have a boyfriend, what's up?"

She dropped her chin and shook her head. "I don't know what you're talking about. Nothing's changed. I'm just the same." She knotted the fingers of her left hand into the napkin in her lap so no one could see she had crossed her fingers again. She'd been doing a lot of that lately.

"Uh huh," he said and then dismissed her. He turned back to his father to talk about what was on hand for business the next week.

He ignored her through the rest of the meal and the trip home again. It was not uncommon, but it stung when his mother followed her into the kitchen once they returned home. "Is something going on?" she asked in a whisper.

"No, Mom. It's just his imagination working overtime today."

Once his parents left two interminable hours later, she retreated to her chair and tried to stay small and silent. If she did not do anything further to earn his wrath, maybe he would forget about his lunchtime accusations.

He settled into his chair with a beer, but instead of focusing on the television, he stared across the room at her. "What was your problem today? You were rude to my parents and made us look bad at the restaurant."

"You were the one yelling," she pointed out, trying not to sound bitter. She turned her attention to the white baby blanket she was knitting for her cousin who was pregnant with her third baby.

"So what the hell's wrong with you? If you weren't hungry you should have stayed at home. That was a damn expensive salad you ate," he pointed out.

She shrugged. "I was hungry, but I didn't see anything I wanted to eat."

"Yeah. Well I'm still full from dinner so I won't need anything else tonight."

She nodded silently, already wondering how she could justify going out and buying a foot long sub to fill the hole in her heart by way of her stomach. But she could not afford to do that, so she settled for two grilled cheese sandwiches and a bowl of tomato soup.

Chapter 7

When she got home on the Friday of her second week of work, there were two messages waiting on the answering machine. "Where have you been?" her mother's voice was half an octave higher than normal. "I've been trying for three days to get hold of you. Are you okay? I've been having a feeling something's wrong. Call me as soon as you can." Click.

She hit the erase button. No need for Matthew to hear that message. He might suspect it had less to do with her mother's bad timing than it did with her not being home to answer the phone. After all, where did she have to go? She was a housewife with no kids to run after and a very few outside activities to occupy her time. That message might reinforce his suspicion that she had a boyfriend.

She was convinced that Matthew thought she spent her days propped in a corner of the kitchen just waiting for his return so she could jump into action and take care of his every need. She had been at work for two full weeks and he still did not suspect a thing. Thank God.

The second message was from Laura at the library. "I just wanted to remind you about the meeting of the newsletter committee next Wednesday. See you at nine." Click.

Picking up the phone, she called Laura back first. Of course she got the older woman's answering machine. At 81 Laura was still a social butterfly. "Hi Laura. I'm afraid I'm going to miss the meeting on Wednesday. I don't think I'll be able to help any more," she said before a heavy mantle of guilt landed on her shoulders. "I think it would be best if you took my name off the committee list. Thanks, good bye."

She clicked the phone off and turned to her chore list. Friday meant leftovers for dinner, changing the sheets on the bed and finishing another load or two of laundry. She had stripped the bed that morning and washed a load of laundry before going to work. Just before she left, she'd put that load into the dryer and a second load into the washer.

It was time to advance the laundry through the next stage of the cycle and take the sheets from the dryer to remake the bed. Then she would walk through the house and make sure things were still presentable before sitting down with a large glass of iced tea.

Though her life had the added dimension of a job, nothing else had changed. Matthew still ignored her, unless he was demanding something. The weekend passed in a blur of gardening and chores she and Matthew did together. It wasn't until Sunday evening that her mother called while she was preparing dinner.

"Hi Mom," she said, picking up the portable phone and propping it between ear and shoulder while she finished slicing a tomato for their salad.

"How did you know it was me?" her mother asked.

"No one else calls at dinnertime on Sunday evening," she said with a smile.

Matthew was outside watching the grill, the only time he cooked. Which was one of the reasons she never learned how to work the grill, though he had offered several times to teach her.

She did not want to learn how to use the small gas grill. If she learned, then he would never help with any of the meals.

"Where have you been? I tried several times last week to call you, but you were never home," her mother complained.

"Why didn't you leave a message before Friday? I would have called you back. I thought you were calling just to chat," she said as she added green peppers and sprinkled grated cheese over the salad. She did not answer the question, but her mother would never realize it.

"I did want to chat, but you weren't home. Where have you been all week?"

She sighed and wondered how best to break the news to her mother or if she should even tell her of the job. Mom was a wild card. She would either be happy and helpful or she would demand to talk to Matthew and let the canary out of the birdcage.

Pulling a nickel from her pocket, she flipped it into the air, then trapped it on the counter before it rolled off onto the floor. *Heads I tell her, tails I don't.* She picked up her hand to reveal the coin and sighed in relief. Tails.

"I've just been out a lot. It's been hectic at the library getting ready for the new school year and all."

Mom would accept that. She was the one who had encouraged her to volunteer at the library.

"Yes, I'm sure you've been busy. I've got to run. Your father's taking me out to dinner tonight and I still have to get dressed."

"Love you, Mom," she said, feeling guilty for not sharing her decisions and her secrets. There would be plenty of time later on to tell her parents. She still had a lot of time before she would leave. In the meantime, she had improvements to implement at the office and a lot of money to save up.

"I love you, too, Honey. Take care of yourself," her mother said before hanging up.

She put the phone in the charger cradle and was carrying the salads to the table when Matthew came in the back door carrying the plate of steaks.

"I think I overcooked yours again," he said.

Of course you did. You always do. You can't seem to understand that meat continues to cook even after its been removed from the grill.

"I don't know what happens. The damn things go from rare to done in like ten seconds," he said, dropping the smaller steak on her plate and trading the plate at his place for the platter in his hands.

"Uh huh," she replied. She bowed her head and said a very short, silent prayer before eating, ignoring Matthew who had dug right into his food.

Cutting into her steak, she took the first bite and tried not to make a face. At least the marinade she used had flavored it well. The meat itself was too overcooked and dry for her taste, though she should be used to it by now. After all, the only time she got a steak to her liking was when she ordered one in a restaurant.

* * * * *

She lay awake for hours that night, wishing, dreaming and planning. Though she had had her job for two full weeks, she had been too intimidated to ask when payday was. She did not mind. She did not have anywhere to put the check when they gave it to her. They could hold onto her money indefinitely as far as she was concerned. Eventually they would remember to pay her, but she did not want to nag them about needing money. She did enough of that at home.

Every month she had to beg Matthew to write her a check for the household checking account while he was paying all the other monthly bills. One month she forgot. Two days later when she asked for the money, he looked at her like she was crazy.

"I gave you a check," he said. His tone was accusatory as if he thought she was trying to take more than his tight-fisted budgeting would allow.

"You have not given me anything this month. If you don't believe me, look at your checkbook."

"You've got to remind me of these things, honey. I have a lot on my mind and can't remember everything," he said as he pulled out his checkbook. "I'm kinda short this month, but this should be enough if you're careful," he said, writing a check.

She stared at the paper when he handed it to her. Fifty dollars. He'd given her fifty dollars to cover five hundred dollars worth of expenses. How was she supposed to budget on that? "Matthew, I need the rest of the money. There's no way I can run the house for a month on fifty dollars."

"Sure you can. You'll just have to be creative. After all, I pay the real bills. So you have to skip your manicure this month. Your fingers won't fall off." Without letting her speak, he headed for the back door. "I'm going to rent a movie."

She didn't even get the chance to argue. She wanted to tell him that the money he gave her went for food and toiletries and the cleaners. He demanded his white button-down oxfords be laundered and pressed professionally each time he wore them. She did her own occasional manicures and pedicures and trimmed the ends of her own hair.

The following month had been extra stressful on her. Every time she turned around she was explaining again why they were eating soup and sandwiches or experimental casseroles. Thank goodness she kept the pantry well stocked.

The final insult came when she had three dollars in the bank and a pile of white oxfords that needed to be laundered. She washed and ironed them and returned them to his closet without a word. The next morning he threw a twenty-minute temper tantrum about her inability to press the sleeves properly and how unpresentable the shirts were.

"I'm sorry, but the money you gave me is gone. I have no money in the household budget for a cleaning bill this month," she said before locking herself in the bathroom. He stood outside the door and continued his tirade about her management capabilities and how ugly his shirts were. She finally turned on the taps in both the sink and tub to drown him out. The running water also covered the sounds of her sobs.

That afternoon he handed her a check for $1000. "This is for the rest of the month and an emergency fund. Do not let this happen again."

She never did. The minute she saw him pull out the bills, she got in line with her hand out for the household money first. Over the last two years, the emergency fund had dwindled to about fifty dollars because of the rising costs of everything except her monthly allowance.

Matthew snorted in his sleep and rolled over, pulling her from her thoughts. When he rolled, he pulled the covers with him so she was only half covered by the red and black silk comforter. This was nothing new. She poked his shoulder and pulled on the corner of the comforter until she'd pulled back enough to cover herself. She rolled to face the wall, keeping a tight grip on the blanket.

If I'm making $600 a week, it should only take three or four months to get enough together so I can leave. But where will I go? What will I do with my life then? How will I live?

Chapter 8

On Tuesday morning, Cody was waiting in the office when she arrived a few minutes before nine.

"Good morning," she said as she went about what had become her morning open the office routine.

"Yeah," he grunted. She was surprised by the greeting. About her third day she figured out that Cody was not a morning person.

After setting a six-pack of Diet Pepsi on her desk, she turned on the computer and took the phone off call forwarding. Then she checked the mailbox on the front porch. Yep, Saturday's mail was still in the ugly metal box by the front door. Back inside again, she stopped at the 55-gallon metal drum they used as a garbage can. She flipped through the mail and tossed the junk into the can. That left only three letters. Two bills for JJ who was the money person and what looked like a personal letter for Cody.

She slipped the letters into their baskets. One of her first innovations was a new organizer box that held all the forms the office used in an orderly manner. Three mail baskets - JJ's, Cody's and the basket for outgoing mail sat on top of that box. She kept her head down and did not look at the man watching her every move. Something about his direct gaze caused her nerves to jangle and her mouth to go dry. Thankfully the computer had booted up so she could focus on something other than the fact that Cody intimidated her. She tried to look him in the eye the few times they'd talked, but it felt as if he could see the emotional scars and unhappiness she kept caged deep inside.

"We owe you a paycheck," Cody said once she'd settled behind her desk.

"Uh huh," she replied, not sure if he was asking a question or making an observation.

"Payday is every other Monday. JJ will make sure your check is ready. Sometimes I forget to give them out. You're doing a great job," he said as he pushed out of the chair he'd been lounging in. "If you ever want to share those heavy thoughts you carry around, I'd be glad to listen and help if I can," he said softly. He slid an envelope across her desk. The white business size envelope had her name printed across the front in bold black letters.

"Thanks for the offer. You've already helped more than I can say," she said, still staring at her computer monitor.

"I'll be at the courthouse if you need me. JJ's upstairs," he said before grabbing the briefcase the two men shared and strolling out.

She watched until he was out of sight. Only then did she turn her attention to the envelope on her desk. Using the antique Bowie knife they used as a letter-opener, she slit the top of the envelope open and with her heart pounding, she pulled out the first paycheck she'd earned since shortly after marrying Matthew.

The amount printed on the check wasn't what she expected. Of the $600 she'd earned in the last two weeks, her check was for only about two-thirds of the total. She checked the envelope for cash or a second check, but only found a small yellow index card. She pulled the card out and read it. Understanding dawned. She might do all the work, but the government took its share before she received the first penny, whether or not she liked it.

With a sigh, she put the check back in the envelope, then put the envelope in her purse. She would go after work and open a bank account so she could start saving for her future. Pulling out the phone book, she opened the yellow pages to "banks." She read through the listings, lost and overwhelmed by such a decision. How did one choose a bank?

Matthew swore by Wachovia. She didn't want her money in the same bank as their joint accounts. She wanted her own money in her own bank. Problem was, she didn't know anything about the other banks in the area. Pulling her paycheck out again, she noticed that "the bosses," as she thought of them, used the local credit union. Knowing JJ and his super-anal tendencies, he had thoroughly investigated the bank before opening any account with them. If it was good enough for the business, it was good enough for her. Checking the phone book, she jotted down the bank's address and phone number on the back of her pay envelope. Then she put the envelope back in her purse and turned to the stack of work on her desk. She would stop by the credit union on her way to the grocery store that afternoon.

* * * * *

By 4:15 she was near tears with frustration. She had arrived at the bank an hour earlier and had been waiting ever since. Every time it looked like one of the bank officers in their glassed-in offices looked free, someone came in who claimed to have an appointment. When she'd called at lunchtime, the receptionist told her she did not need an appointment, that they always had someone free to help new customers.

The plastic formed chairs were the most uncomfortable things she had ever experienced and finally she could take it no more.

She would come back later in the week. For today, she wanted to cash her check. She got in the fast moving line for the tellers and in minutes was standing in front of one of the tired looking women.

"How can I help you?" the woman asked. She sounded like a working woman who was trying to juggle too much in her life.

"I'd like to cash this check, please," she said, sliding the document across the wide white chest-high counter that separated them.

"Do you have an account here?" the teller asked.

"No, but the check is drawn on this bank," she pointed out, her tension level ratcheting up another notch.

"There will be a three-dollar charge to cash a check for a non-account holder," the teller said.

"Three dollars? To give me money you already have in this bank?" she asked, incredulous.

"If you had an account here, there wouldn't be a charge," the teller said as if reading off a prompter card.

"I've been sitting over there for an hour waiting for someone to open an account for me. Now I have to give you money so I can get my money so I can get home and try to figure out how and when I will be able to get back here to open an account," she ground out. She had had enough. As she growled at the teller, tears began rolling from her eyes.

"I'm sorry, but the charge is bank policy. Do you want me to cash the check or would your rather come back another day?"

"I'll come back," she said, wiping away her tears and trying to calm herself. Somehow she would find a way to cash the damn check without having to pay a service fee or spending another hour waiting for someone to help her.

She stuffed the check and ID back into her purse as she walked out of the bank. She was cutting it close, but she should be able to get to the grocery store and home before Matthew, if the stars were shining luck in her direction.

Only, as usual, luck was not to be hers. She only picked up the few necessities to get through; toilet paper, potato chips, milk, a 6-pack of beer for Matthew and pot pies for dinner, but the checkout lines were slow as a Carolina hound in July. Once she reached the clerk, she had to search for her driver's license to prove that she was over 21. Of course, it was not in her wallet. She had taken it out at the bank, but where had she put it?

Think girl. You had it ten minutes ago, where did you put it?

She checked the pockets of her slacks and the pockets of her purse. Just when she was about to give up on the beer, she closed her eyes, took a deep breath and tried to remember. She did not have time to backtrack to the bank for her driver's license. She could not have left it behind.

The bank teller had laid it on top of the check before sliding both across the counter to her. Fumbling in the main compartment of her purse, she pulled out the envelope and riffled through the contents until she found the plastic card that validated her existence as a legal member of society.

"Here it is," she said, handing the card to the clerk. The young woman barely glanced it before handing it back.

It took a few more minutes for the mentally challenged young man to bag her groceries, but she was soon on her way home. She should arrive ten minutes before Matthew. That would give her plenty of time to get the groceries put away. He would never be the wiser about her crappy afternoon, or her job.

* * * *

As soon as she pulled in the driveway she knew there was going to be trouble. Matthew was home early. He was on the riding lawnmower circling the backyard. The front yard was already finished. He'd even edged the front walk and along the curbs before moving to the backyard.

Taking a deep breath for courage, she climbed from the car, pulling the grocery bags out with her. She was halfway to the house when the lawnmower engine silenced. She kept walking as if it were normal for her to be gone most of the afternoon.

He caught up with her at the back door. "Where have you been all afternoon? I took off early so we could go and do something."

"It's Tuesday. You usually take off early on Friday," she pointed out.

"I thought we could go to the matinee of that movie you wanted to see. So I took off early," he said.

"I'm sorry," she replied. "If I'd known, I would have changed my plans. You should have told me."

"I called this morning. Where have you been all day? The message was still on the machine when I came home at one," he said, sounding like a little boy whose dog had run away from home, then returned home two days later, pregnant and guilty.

"I went to Jacksonville," she said, wondering how she was going to keep up the secrecy of her job. She never went to Jacksonville.

"Jacksonville? Why?"

She did not answer immediately. Instead, she put the groceries away, turned on the oven and pulled out the cookie sheet from the drawer under the stove.

"I'm waiting," he said, now sounding like her father had the night she stayed out two hours past her midnight curfew the night she graduated from high school.

Pushing past him to get to the stove she finally said, "If you must know, I went to Michael's to see what new craft stuff they have. Then I went to the mall and wandered around. After a late lunch at Red Lobster, I came home by way of the Emerald Isle bookstore and the Food Lion. If you need to see receipts to verify my whereabouts, you're outta luck. I didn't buy anything except groceries."

As she created a day she would like to spend, she slid the pot pies out of their boxes onto a cookie tray. She slid the tray into the oven, slammed the door shut, set the timer then turned and walked out of the kitchen. Surprisingly, he did not follow her.

With one hand, she rubbed at the burning in her stomach. With the other, she wiped away the tear that popped from nowhere to roll down her left cheek. She did not stop until she was in the master bath. After locking the door, she stripped and stepped into the shower. She released the frustration of the afternoon and her resentment of Matthew's questions in a flurry of gut-clenching sobs that doubled her over under the spray of hot water.

It was a violent, though brief, release. By the time she turned the water off and reached for a towel a few minutes later, she had herself back under control. A bit of cool water splashed on her cheeks and eyelids, a bit of moisturizing cream on her face and neck and she was ready for what she was sure would be round two of the "discussion." Surely he would not accept her explanation that easily. He would want to pick it to pieces, analyze every second of her day as he had in the past when she had gone somewhere alone. She would have to hang tough, keep her answers simple and not collapse under the pressure. She could not tell him about her job.

She was surprised when nothing more was said. He finished cutting the grass, ate dinner and took a shower before settling in for Tuesday night television. She retreated to her corner of the couch across the room where she wrote a long letter to Nikki about her job and the dreams for her future. Then she sat and tried to figure out exactly how long it would take to earn the money she needed and how to earn extra money so she could afford to live on her own. She did not want to have to depend on Matthew for anything, even though she should be due alimony. She wanted her freedom more than she wanted Matthew's money.

As she lay her head on the pillow later that evening, JJ's offer to train her as a bail enforcement agent popped into her thoughts. All at once she was wide-awake again. A dozen questions crowded into her thoughts, leading to a dozen more. If only she had pad and paper to write them all down. She would be up all night thinking of things to ask Cody and JJ about training and work and hours and possibilities. But it was late and her bad day dragged on her.

Tomorrow was another day. She would think of questions at work and try to engage JJ in a discussion of whether or not their offer to train her had been legitimate or just a way to get her to organize the office. She had other things to discuss with JJ as well. The top priority was a second cell phone or a beeper system. Twice in the last week when she'd called the cell phone, she woke Cody. He growled then clicked the phone off. After the second time it happened, she spent two hours online shopping and comparing cell phone plans and providers, trying to come up with a workable solution that would not be too expensive. She had no idea what the company finances were like, but figured they had to be tight. Cody and JJ were doing all the work on renovating the house themselves and had not brought in a team to get the job done fast. That would have been Matthew's way.

She was not sure which approach she would take, hiring the job out or doing it herself. Watching the downstairs hallway and unfinished rooms take shape was exciting, even though she had not done any of the work. She could always count on a major advance in the renovation when she reported for work on Monday morning. Smaller jobs were finished during the week, but major strides were taken on the weekends when "the bosses" did not have to report for court and only responded to jail calls, which usually came in the early morning hours.

* * * * *

By morning, she questioned her sanity. Did she want to get beaten up by someone not wanting to go to jail? Maybe she should take some classes at the Community College and train to be something that earned more money than a secretary. But what?

She had never thought about what she wanted to be when she grew up. Though out of fashion, her mother had taught her that a woman's role was to take care of those around her. A career outside the home was for other women. When she married Matthew, he agreed with her mother and insisted she stay at home and take care of him. She never thought a time would come when she would need a job or a career of her own.

After dealing with the day's paperwork and calling their clients to remind them of their court dates for the following day, she pulled out her notes on cell phone rates and plans. She spent the rest of the day playing with the spreadsheet program and putting together what she thought was a damn good argument for the business investing in a new phone plan with multiple lines and unlimited minutes, local and nationwide. Once she'd saved the file, she used the word processing program to write a lengthy memo outlining her arguments. She printed out three copies of each page; one for each boss and one for a file she created to hold all the supporting notes and documentation.

Once she was finished with that, she typed a note listing a few of the biggest questions she had about being a bail enforcement agent. She only printed two copies of that file. She put one in her desk, then stood looking at the two men's in-boxes for a long time, debating who would be more responsive to her questions.

Still debating, she laid it on her desk while she shut the office down for the night. The phone rang and when she finished answering the hysterical mother's questions about bailing her son out of jail, it was past time to go home.

She felt good as she climbed into her car that day. She was making a difference, even if it was only in the lives of her employers. She was earning her paycheck. She was no longer the worthless blob Matthew often accused her of becoming.

Chapter 9

"What does your husband have to say about you becoming an enforcement agent?" Cody asked the next morning after she opened the office. He tossed aside the paper he had been reading while she went through her morning routine. She glanced down and saw that he had been reading her list of questions.

She tried to maintain eye contact with him, but had to glance away time and again to look over his shoulder, out the window, anywhere but in those piercing eyes. He saw too much when she met his gaze. She swallowed hard and dropped her gaze to her hands. The two gold bands on her left ring finger were nicked and scratched. The one-third carat diamond winked at her as if it knew a secret.

Raising her head she straightened her shoulders. She forced herself to meet his inquisitive gaze. "He doesn't know I'm thinking about it."

"Don't you think you should talk to him?" Cody asked. He sounded surprised that she kept such a decision to herself.

"Why? It's none of his business," she said, sounding bitter even to herself. She fought the urge to duck under her desk.

Cody's gaze sharpened. His eyes narrowed for few seconds while he studied her. Then he relaxed and picked up his travel mug. "Does he hit you? Hurt you? Beat on you?"

"No," she said, dropping her gaze again. Her fingers were knotted together on top of the desk. "He's never raised a hand to me. He's never had to. His words do enough damage." She jumped when a tear landed on her fingers, wet and burning hot. Talking about the failing relationship added to the pain instead of detracting from it.

"You should leave him if he hurts you, even if he only uses words," Cody said, his deep voice gentler than she ever heard before.

"I plan to. But it takes money to start over. Apartments, divorces and just plain living cost money," she pointed out, wiping away her tears with shaking fingers. "He doesn't know I'm working. I hope to save my paychecks for a few months until I have enough to leave," she said, outlining her goal. "Problem is, I'll probably need a second job once I'm on my own. I thought you could train me to be a bail enforcement agent. That way I'll be able to support myself once I leave Matthew by working here and doing bail enforcement as well."

She glanced up when Cody stood. His expression chilled her to the bone. He turned and stalked from the room. She stood to follow until she heard a string of inventive curses, which stopped her in her tracks. She stopped halfway across the room. Her shoulders drew up as if she were a turtle pulling into its shell. Her arms wrapped around her middle to protect herself and then the shaking began. Cody was mad and it was her fault.

What would he do? Would he call Matthew and share her secret? Or hunt him down and hold a "come to Jesus" meeting about how to treat a woman?

She found herself barely breathing as she waited for Cody to calm down. Would he fire her? Or just yell at her for being stupid?

When the back door slammed and glass shattered, she jumped. She rushed into the hall that ran down the center of the house. Cody was standing outside the back door looking at her through the hole where glass had been just moments before.

She froze mid step, waiting for a second explosion. In her experience men who did something as destructive as shattering a window never dealt well with the aftermath. Before she could apologize his lips stretched into a wide grin and then he began to chuckle.

She stared at him, afraid to move. Matthew often smiled too, just before attacking her with a verbal backhand. When she got upset at his words, he would take offense. "I was only teasing," he'd say. "You really need to learn how to take a joke."

But his insults were not jokes. They were degrading, belittling, cutting comments. With each slap, each insult, she faded, eventually becoming the human doormat Matthew walked upon on a regular basis.

"Are you all right?" she asked in a small voice. She braced herself for anger.

"I'm fine, but JJ was right. That old door didn't survive my temper. Could you wake him up and tell him to go buy a new door? I'll clean the glass up later."

She nodded. As he turned away, she called, "I'm sorry."

Cody paused, then turned back to face her. He looked serious, somber, but not angry. "Why are you sorry? I broke the glass," he said. "I've got to get to the courthouse. This afternoon the three of us will sit down and talk about a training schedule."

"Training schedule?"

"Yeah, we've got to get you in shape and trained to help us track down the bad guys."

Before she could ask anything further, he disappeared around the building. She retrieved the broom and dustpan from the newly renovated kitchen. As she began to sweep up, the front door opened. Looking up, she watched Cody stalk into the office and emerge a moment later carrying the court briefcase. Neither spoke, but when his eyes met hers, she could see he was on her side.

Yeah, you thought Matthew was not like your father either. Did not take too long to find out the two men were more alike than you could ever imagine.

After cleaning up the glass, she slowly climbed the stairs. Until now she had acted like there was a locked door at the bottom of the staircase. The higher she climbed, the less comfortable she became. This was their home. She was not sure she should be up here. She felt like a rabbit who'd been snatched out of the woods and set down in the middle of Time Square.

When she reached the top of the stairs, she paused and looked around. No progress had yet been made in renovating the second floor. The floors had been stripped of carpet. The bare wood was rough, stained in places and several of the narrow boards were missing. The walls were bare, but time had left its mark here as well. In some places, the paint had fallen from the wall, exposing layer upon layer of color, some shades attractive, others nauseating in tone and intensity. The history of decorating could be found on these walls.

She stepped into the hallway and looked up and down, not certain what to do. So she did the only thing she could think of. "JJ!" she screamed at the top of her lungs. "JJ, wake up! There's been an accident!"

She turned to face the staircase. She had not seen a naked man in years, not even Matthew, and was not sure the first should be her boss. Thankfully, when he appeared beside her thirty seconds later, he was wearing cutoff gray sweatpants and a faded blue T-shirt. His feet were bare. In one hand he held a really big handgun.

He looked her up and down, then scanned the staircase. "What?" he asked in a whisper, pulling her back two steps so they were out of view of the front door. "What's wrong?"

Her gaze still glued to the gun she shook her head. "Cody broke the glass in the back door. He wants you to go and buy a new one."

She tore her gaze from the weapon and looked at his face. It took a few seconds, but her words finally penetrated his sleep-fogged brain.

"Cody broke the back door?" JJ shifted and tucked the gun into the back of his shorts. Then he swiped a hand over his face. "I've warned him about taking his anger out on this old house, but he never listens. Okay, I'll get dressed and go buy a new door. With luck I'll have it installed before lunch."

She nodded and turned to head back downstairs but paused. "Can I ask a question?"

JJ smiled at her. He woke quickly once he was on his feet. "You just did."

"Yeah, well, do you have anyone special at the credit union you work with?" Today she was going to call and make an appointment with someone no matter what the phone answerer tried to tell her.

"Why? Do you need a banker?"

"I need to open a savings account and I thought if you had someone special you worked with I would make an appointment with them."

JJ frowned at her. "Why don't you come with me. The credit union is right next to Lowe's. You can open an account while I get the new door."

"What about the office? Will it be all right with the window out and no one here?"

"This is New Bern. It will be fine. Besides, we won't be gone that long." JJ turned to head down the hall. "Give me fifteen minutes and I'll be ready to go."

She nodded and headed back downstairs. As soon as she was back on the first floor, she took a deep breath and felt the knots in her shoulder loosen. Picking up the file with her cell phone information, she decided to talk to JJ about phone plans while they were in his truck.

Chapter 10

Once they were in his big black SUV, she did not know how to start her cell phone presentation. They were halfway across town before she finally muttered, "OBTAD."

"Excuse me?" JJ asked.

She swallowed hard and hoped for courage. "Um, I know I've only worked for you a couple of weeks, but I was wondering if you had ever thought about making some administrative changes?"

"Like what?" he asked. He sounded interested, but skeptical.

"You and Cody each need your own cell phone."

She pulled out the spreadsheet she had put together to refer to and launched into the sales pitch she had been rehearsing. She did not pause until she listed all the benefits of a second phone and the convenience to the two men as well as to the business.

When she finally wound down, she looked around. They were parked in the credit union's parking lot. JJ never said a word to shut her up and was now watching her with an intensity that caused a shiver to run through her. No one had looked at her with such focused attention in more years than she could remember.

"Wow, that was an impressive presentation. The only problem is I'd like you redo it. I want you to compare corporate rates for unlimited minutes, nationwide coverage and three phones. Think you can handle that?"

She nodded, then pulled a pen out of her pocket and made notes on the back of the spreadsheet.

"Come on, I'll introduce you to my favorite banker," JJ said, looking at the bank for a moment. His expression grew somber. He pocketed the keys and exited the SUV.

She followed him and was surprised when he opened the door and held it, waiting for her to pass through ahead of him. For a moment she wondered what the others in the bank thought of them. She was certain the dumpy plain white woman and the buff, gorgeous black man traveling together made an odd sight. Before she grew too self-conscious, JJ touched her shoulder and pointed to the back of the room where an older black woman was working in a glassed-in office. She wore a raspberry-colored suit and had her gray streaked hair styled in a classic bob.

She went where he pointed, her shoulders hunched, chin lowered. She tried to shrink under the stares that followed them across the large room. She slowed, allowing JJ to take the lead. That way she could stare at his tall broad-shouldered form and not have to look at anyone else.

JJ stepped into the office and said, "Aunt Fred, you really need to get a job that does not make you spend all day in a fishbowl."

Startled, the woman behind the desk turned from her computer with a frown that lasted only until she recognized the intruder. Then she broke into a dazzling smile. "JJ!" She jumped out of her chair, rounded the desk and threw herself into his arms.

He caught her and hugged her tight before setting her back on her feet and kissing her cheek.

"So what brings my bank phobic nephew in today?"

"My friend here needs to open an account. I figured you were the lady to see," JJ said as he backed out of the room. "I'll see you later. I have to go buy a door."

"Sunday at the house. The whole family will be there. And bring Cody," Aunt Fred called as he crossed the bank's main lobby, appearing eager to be out of the building. He waved in acknowledgement, but didn't slow down.

She watched, curious as to this side of JJ. He had never been abrupt with her. He always spared her time to answer her questions or deal with any problems she encountered. Was it this place or this woman that made him nervous?

Once he was outside, Aunt Fred turned to look her over. "Come on in. You'd like to open an account? Checking or savings?" The older woman waved her into one of the two chairs in front of her desk. She returned to her oversized executive chair. Nothing more was said about JJ's strange reaction to being in the bank.

She looked around the room in a panic. She did not have a clue. "Can I open a savings account today and come back later to open a checking account?"

"Sure. Once we get your main account set up adding others is easy. The tellers can open them for you. I'll need your driver's license and social security number. We'll have you set up in no time," Aunt Fred reached into a drawer and pulled out a multi-copy form.

In less than ten minutes she was walking out of the bank. She felt so happy she thought she was hovering a few inches above the ground. She crossed the parking lot, clutching her deposit receipt and her brand new ATM card in one hand.

As she headed across the busy 3-lane road that separated the bank from Lowe's Building Center she focused on getting across the street without getting run over. Finally there was a break in traffic. She did not look at the cars as she race-walked the last few yards to the far side of the road.

She found JJ at the exit pushing a large cart with a door on it. After stuffing the bank papers in her purse, she followed him and the door to the SUV. With the help of a couple of men on their way into Lowe's, the door was loaded and they were on their way back to the office. Upon their return, JJ looked from her to the door, then turned and headed inside.

"Aren't we going to unload the door?" she called after him.

JJ turned from the back porch and looked her up and down. "You're great in the office, but I'm gonna need Cody for that job."

She shrugged and started toward him. "Okay. I'll get back to work then. Thanks for helping me open my new account."

"No problem. I'm surprised you didn't have an account already," he said, curiosity in his expression.

She turned away before lifting her shoulders again. "It's a long story and I have to get back to work. My boss wouldn't like the office to be unmanned while I hang out in the parking lot."

JJ grinned, "I bet your boss wouldn't mind too much."

"I don't know. He's a real task master," she grinned back as she opened the door and headed inside.

Chapter 11

She drove home that afternoon feeling invincible. JJ and Cody agreed that with some training, both physical and mental, she would make an unexpected bail enforcement agent. They also agreed that being unusual and unexpected would work in her favor. She stopped at the bookstore on her way home and asked the clerk about books on female bounty hunters.

"Female bounty hunters? You've got to read the Stephanie Plum books. They're incredible," the clerk led the way through the store to the shelf of books she was talking about. "If you want a vampire bounty hunter, the Anita Blake stories are your best bet."

She picked up the first Stephanie Plum book in paperback, promising herself that if she liked it she would come back for the others. After checking out, she finished the drive home, singing along with the car's radio. Life was good and she was going to make it through the next few months. She was going to become strong and self sufficient enough to break the ties of pain that held her tied to Matthew and their sham of a marriage.

Turning into the driveway, she jammed on the breaks and stopped short, missing Matthew's car by only a dozen inches. He had parked in the middle of the driveway at an angle so her car would not fit on either side of his.

Confused and concerned, she backed up and parked on the street. "Wonder what's happened," she murmured to herself as she gathered her purse and the bag from the bookstore. As she climbed from the car, she took several deep breaths and tried to prepare herself for Matthew.

She paused at the back door. "You can do this. Just keep your mouth shut about the job," she whispered to her reflection in the door's window. She opened the door and stepped through, half-expecting Matthew to be waiting just inside, arms folded, foot tapping, staring at his watch. But he was not there.

Dropping her purse and the book on the counter, she crossed the kitchen to the living room. "Matthew?"

He was not in there either. She headed for the bedroom next and was surprised to find a trail of clothes from just outside the bedroom door to the bed.

Matthew was curled up in the middle of the mattress, her pillow in his arms sound asleep. Sweat beaded across his forehead, though the room was cool. She reached out and felt heat radiating from him when her palm was still two inches from his skin. He was burning up.

"Matthew? What's wrong?" she asked, shaking his shoulder gently.

Matthew grunted, opened one eye and looked up at her. "I feel like shit. Can you make me some hot chocolate?"

"Yes," she said, going to the closet and kicking off her loafers.

"And can you bring me some Aspirin?"

"Yes," she said. "Anything else?"

The eye blinked and then looked up at her again. "Where were you? I came home at lunchtime and you weren't here to take care of me."

"I was at the library helping with the newsletter," she said, crossing her fingers behind her back.

"Oh, okay," he said as his eyes drifted closed again.

She changed into jeans and an oversized T-shirt then retrieved water and Aspirin from the bathroom. She woke Matthew again and helped him take the tablets with several swallows of water. As soon as she released him, he rolled over, curled up and drifted off again.

Without Matthew to demand Thursday's meatloaf dinner, she decided to make herself a ham and cheese sandwich. Afterward, she put on her sneakers and headed out for a power-walk through the neighborhood. Years ago she'd mapped out a two-mile course and now decided the best way to get in shape was to walk it every evening after dinner.

Though JJ and Cody had assured her that being a BEA was not about strength, she was not so sure. In any case, she knew she needed to be in better shape than she was right now, even if she never got as buff as her employers. She wanted, just once, to run the bad guy down and tackle him like on television. Now that would be a brave thing day.

As she walked, she allowed her daydreams to go wild. She envisioned herself slim, trim and able to handle anything thrown her way. She saw herself in a few months in an apartment with a friendly, though protective, dog. Her apartment would be her haven, a place that she would decorate all by herself, though she was not sure what kind of décor she would want. She did know it would be as far from glass and chrome, black, red and silver, as she could get.

By the time she returned home, she has come up with several more things to add to her to do list. Add extra exercise to her daily routine. Research decorating and what styles she liked. Look into apartments and find a neighborhood where she felt safe and comfortable.

The first thing she did on entering the kitchen was to pour a large glass of iced tea. After kicking off her sneakers, she headed to the living room. She needed to sit for a few minutes and recover. Though she had made it through the full two-mile loop, she was worn out.

Matthew was slumped in his chair watching a sit-com. He was wearing a pair of navy blue silk boxers and a white T-shirt.

"Feel better?" she asked as she settled in her chair across the room.

"Where have you been? I got up and you weren't here. There's nothing for dinner." He sounded like a sick, tired, grumpy little boy.

"I went for a walk. Are you feeling better?"

"I guess. I'm kinda hungry," He burped, yawned and scratched, no longer embarrassed about performing such actions in front of her. When had he stopped being conscious of such behavior? With a sigh he settled deeper into his recliner.

"I had a sandwich. How about I fix you some soup and a sandwich?"

"Grilled cheese?"

"If you'd like."

"Hot chocolate? And chicken noodle soup?"

She nodded, fighting the urge to throw a salute his way. Carrying her tea with her, she headed for the kitchen. His requests turned her stomach when combined together, but whenever he was sick this was what he wanted. Once everything was heated, she carried it to the living room. Tonight he would not move from his recliner except to go to the bathroom or back to bed.

"Where were you today?" he asked as she set the tray in his lap then returned to the kitchen for the forgotten napkin and soupspoon.

"I told you earlier, I was at the library folding newsletters," she said.

Was he so sick that he would be home from work for more than one day? How would she handle that? She had only been working for a few weeks, how could she ask for a day off?

"Funny, I checked the mail when I got home and the library newsletter was in the mail. There was a note inside from some woman saying they were sorry you had to stop helping, but they appreciated all you'd done in the past." Matthew said. "What's going on with you? You're never home anymore, you're humming and now you're exercising. You're lying about something. Are you fooling around on me?"

"No, I'm not fooling around on you," she said her brain scrambling for some logical explanation.

"Then what the hell's going on? Mom stopped by the office this morning and said she stopped by the other day and you weren't home then either."

She looked away, growing still and small. His tone became accusatory and angry, a deadly combination she knew from past experience. If she did not answer him soon, he would launch into one of his "discussions," tearing her apart and telling her all the things that were wrong with her. And the last thing she needed right now was Matthew listing all of her faults.

"So? Where were you?"

"I was at work, okay? I got a job and I was working."

Silence dropped over the room like a bomb. Even the television grew silent as a public service announcement for the deaf came on. Matthew sat in his chair unmoving, unblinking. She was not sure he was even breathing.

This was it, the moment she had been dreading since taking the leap and finding the job. But the secret was out and she would deal with Matthew here and now. These next few moments would be her OBTAD. She took a deep breath and lifted her chin a fraction of an inch. One thing she had learned over the last weeks was that she was much stronger than she ever realized. Matthew's assessment of her being a pathetic church mouse might have been true once upon a time, but now she was a mouse with the beginnings of a backbone. No matter what he said, she was going to keep her job and save her money for her future.

Finally Matthew blinked. "You what?"

"I got a job," she said. No need to get any more specific for now. Not until he demanded it.

"But you don't know how to do anything," he said. "How long have you had this job?" he asked, moving from shock to suspicion.

"A couple of weeks," she said, remaining informative, but not effusive in her explanation.

"And what are you doing in this new job?" the suspicion grew.

"I'm a secretary for two businessmen." Secretary sounded less impressive than office manager and she would never admit to the job she hoped was in her future.

"Why didn't you tell me before now? You didn't have to lie about it," Matthew moved from suspicion to pouting. "I'm really proud that you found a job. I don't understand why you felt you couldn't tell me." All at once he sounded like a proud father whose child had taken their first steps. It sounded like he had done something wonderful, not her.

She did not say anything. She could not tell him the truth. She was tired of lying. Saying nothing seemed the best route to take. But it did not help the guilt that mushroomed in her gut.

He did not notice her silence. "Of course, you can't keep it," he continued. All at once he was no longer sick. He pushed out of his chair with a grunt, then began to pace the room.

"Why not? It's just a little part-time job. It hasn't stopped me from keeping the house running smoothly. You didn't even know I was working until I told you," she pointed out.

She winced when she heard the note of whininess in her voice. She was losing control, giving up already. Guilt was taking over. If she lost control now he would win and she would be trapped in this emotional hell forever.

Taking a deep breath, she fought to regain calm. Her life, her future depended on this conversation. She had to stay strong and in control. Otherwise he would win.

"No, you'll have to quit. My wife can't work. What will the neighbors think?" Matthew paced back and forth in front of the huge picture window in his boxer shorts. "They'll think I can't take care of my family, my responsibilities," he continued without giving her a chance to respond.

"I'm not quitting. I like my job. I'm good at my job. I'm keeping my job," she said, pushing out of her own chair, grabbing her Stephanie Plum book and started across the living room.

She needed to get away from him before something happened. She could feel the door that held her emotions in check bulging outward, trying to burst open. If that happened, she would scream, rage, cry and tell him all the things she had suppressed over the last ten years. Of course he would not listen to her. He would not hear anything except her near hysterical tone and that would make him defensive. Then he would attack with all the things he thought was wrong with her and cut off her emotional growth before it really had a chance to sink its roots.

She had to stay calm, stay logical and stick to her guns. She would keep this job. She had to keep this job. The rest of her life depended on the next few minutes.

"Of course you're quitting. My wife will not work."

She got to the kitchen door and turned to look at him. All at once she was feeling very, very brave. "I will work and you will get over it. If the neighbors say anything to you, tell them I've gone crazy and you can't control my actions any longer."

With that she went to the kitchen, slipped on her sneakers, grabbed her purse and walked out the back door. She climbed into her car and drove away, not giving in to tears until she was several blocks from the house.

Chapter 12

When her tears subsided and she got herself back under control, she put the car in gear and drove on. She did not know where she was going; she just allowed the car to go where it would. She had no real friends she could drop in on and share her troubles with. She did not drink so going to a bar was a waste of time and energy. Besides, she did not want to be upbeat and friendly. She was tired of keeping her emotional façade erected so the world thought she was content in her life and her marriage.

When she finally looked around and paid attention to her surroundings, she was parked in front of C&JJ Bail Bonds. Dusk was falling. The courthouse parking lot was empty and there was no one else parked up and down the block. She was alone and felt lonelier than ever before.

The lights were on inside the office as well as in every room on the second floor, but she did not move. Her hands were still wrapped around the steering wheel and gripping it so tight that the muscles in her arms were cramping. She was not sure what would happen if she let go. It was as if by holding on to that circular piece of plastic over steel, she could stay in control of her life.

Night eased down around the car. Darkness veiled her from the occasional police car that drove by on their way to or from the courthouse. She had no idea how long she sat, staring at the lights on Broad Street, watching the signal at the corner of Broad and Craven cycle green-yellow-red, green-yellow-red.

She jumped when the driver's door opened, her eyes closing against the interior light that flashed on. But she did not move. She kept hold on the wheel, the need for freedom and the guilty anger that arguing with Matthew always left her with fighting for dominance.

"You okay?" The voice was a familiar one, but not one she wanted to hear just then. She was not ready to face anyone yet. She was not sure she would be ready to face anyone ever again. The gentleness of the gruff voice ripped right through the paper-thin wall she had been struggling to reinforce around her sadness, her anger and her resentment.

"No," she whispered. Tears began to roll down her cheeks, but she couldn't wipe them away. She could not let go of the steering wheel.

"You've been out here quite a while. Why don't you come inside?" Cody sounded nervous. Why was he nervous? Had he never dealt with a crazy woman before?

She had to be crazy if she thought she could break away from Matthew and make a life of her own. "I don't know why I came here. I'm sorry," she said, her voice breaking. Tears continued to roll down her cheeks.

"Why don't we go inside. We can have a beer and talk about it. If you stay out here much longer, the cops are going to start asking questions."

With a watery sigh, she nodded and released the steering wheel. She was only slightly surprised when the world did not fly away like a blown up balloon with a pinhole in it. She climbed from the car, pocketed her keys and allowed Cody to lead the way inside. There was banging coming from the second floor, but he ignored it and headed for the kitchen. She followed slowly, still caught in the whirlpool of emotions that raged through her.

"Drink this and follow me," he said. He handed her a green bottle, then guided her back down the hall and up the stairs. He carried several more beers in his hands.

"You're not drinking," her observed when she stopped at the top of the stairs.

She lifted the bottle and took several swallows, her brain still on overload. It was not until the third swallow that the taste of beer hit her and she realized what she was doing. Swallowing hard, she lowered the bottle and pulled a face at the taste. "Happy?"

"Finish that and then we'll talk. Do you know how to use a crowbar?"

Frowning, she shrugged. Matthew had never allowed her access to any tool bigger than a screwdriver and that had been years ago. Admitting that would only bring more questions she was not ready to answer yet.

Cody took her arm and led her into a room at the far back corner of the house from the office. Once upon a time this might have been a bedroom. Now it was a disaster area. JJ stood in the middle of the room with debris all around him staring at the wall. Only the wall was gone and only the interior studs were left standing.

"Where have you been? I could have used a hand with that last section of wall," he said before turning to his partner. "Hello, is it morning already?"

She had to smile. The man with skin the color of fine milk chocolate was covered head to toe with sweat and dust. He looked like he should be in one of those zombie movies Matthew loved to watch.

"No, it's not morning yet. But I found that extra pair of hands you said we needed for the other wall," Cody handed him a beer.

He stuck the others in a bucket of ice in the corner. Turning in her direction, he nodded to the bottle in her hand. "If you're not used to it, beer goes down better when it's cold."

She looked away and raised the bottle. This time she drank several swallows took a breath, then chugged down the rest. Pulling the bottle from her lips, she took another deep breath and opened her mouth to ask where she could put the empty. Only she never got the question out. Instead, a long, loud burp erupted and echoed around the room.

Before either man could stop her, she whirled and raced from the room. She was halfway down the stairs when the first swallow of beer slammed into her brain. Her legs went boneless. Her knees crumbled and she sat down hard on the stairs. Tears burned their way out of her eyes and down her cheeks. She sniffed and folded into herself, burying her face into her knees. She still held the beer bottle in one hand. The other one she raised and covered her mouth, trying to hold back the sobs. But they refused to be squashed any longer.

Someone settled next to her, but she could not stop crying. A moment later the empty bottle was pulled from her grasp and a cold, wet one replaced it. "If you'd like, we can beat him to a pulp for you," Cody offered.

Not raising her head off her arms, she shook it from side to side. "He's the kind who would have you arrested for assault and then sue you for damages."

Taking a deep breath, she felt an unrecognized warmth surge through her. That warmth pushed down all the useless anger, guilt and overwhelming sadness that had been kept unacknowledged in her for so many years. The negative emotions drained away, as if seeping out her toes, skittering down the stairs and out the front door like the black ooze from an old X-Files episode. The vivid image brought a smile to her lips and dried her overactive tear ducts.

"Want to talk about it?" For the second time since she had met him, Cody sounded tentative.

"My husband demanded I quit my job. He does not want me

to work because he says the neighbors will think badly of him," she said. Her voice sounded dull, lifeless even though she felt life stirring deep in her gut for the first time in recent memory.

"So are you?" JJ asked from the top of the stairs. He sounded worried.

"No, This is my job and I'm keeping it. I told him that just before I walked out."

"Good for you," JJ said.

"So what can we do?" Cody asked when she did not say anything further.

She took a deep breath and sat up. She wiped her hands over her face and sniffed. "Give me a hammer and let me beat on that wall for awhile." She looked at Cody, holding the gaze for more than five seconds. She did not blink or look away until he nodded.

"All right," he said, "let's go beat on a wall."

For the next few hours she drank several more beers, helped tear down the offending wall and helped clean up the resulting debris. She felt more confident than ever about her job and her future. She did not leave until after three, and then only after passing JJ's version of a roadside sobriety test. She had to walk backwards, then balance on one foot and sing silly songs.

Once it was determined she was safe to drive, both men walked her out to her car. She promised to be back the next morning, but JJ shook his head. "Come in at noon."

She drove home hyperalert to the use of traffic signals and speed limits. She saw no one else on her drive home. No police, no other cars, not even a dog. It was as if she were the only one left alive in town. For a moment she toyed with the image of zombies lining up and chasing her across town.

When she got home, she stopped in the bathroom long enough to brush dust from her hair, brush her teeth and wipe down with a wet washcloth. She would shower in the morning. Right now she needed to sleep. After pulling on her nightshirt, she slipped into bed and curled up. As she lay with Matthew snoring behind her, she smiled into the dark. She was exhausted, but felt stronger than she had in ages, both physically and emotionally. With a deep sigh of near contentment, she relaxed into sleep. She did not think about what the morning might bring.

Chapter 13

She woke the next morning to a sharp jab in the middle of her back from Matthew's elbow as he scrambled from bed. "Oh God, I overslept again. Why didn't the alarm go off? Why didn't you wake me up?"

She didn't bother to point out that he had just woken her up. It would have been a waste of energy. Since she felt like she had closed her eyes just five minutes before, she did not have energy to spare.

"Forget fixing me a pot of coffee, could you just zap a cup of instant?" Matthew called from the bathroom as he turned on the shower.

Again she did not answer, but did pry her eyes open and frown at the wall while she took inventory. She had a thick feeling to her tongue. Her sinuses felt like they were packed with wet cotton. But there was no headache. That surprised her, but she was certain it would hit her as soon as she sat up.

She left the bed in stages. First she swung her legs over the side and pushed into a sitting position. She raised her arms and stretched before reaching for her sweatpants. After pulling them up as far as her thighs, she planted her feet on the floor and stood before pulling them on the rest of the way. She waited for a morning after hangover migraine to slam home, reminding her of the events of the previous evening. Only stiffness and tightness in her arms, legs and back reminded her of the physical labor she had engaged in the night before.

She used the half bath downstairs and tried not to look in the mirror. It was way too early to scare herself with that vision. She needed caffeine first. Running her fingers through her waist length hair to push it out of her face, she headed to the kitchen. In seconds Matthew's coffee mug in the microwave and she had retrieved a Pepsi from the vegetable crisper drawer. With a sigh, she popped the can open, lifted it to her lips and drank straight from the can. She consumed half the contents in a few swallows. When she lowered the can, she burped none to delicately and sighed again when she felt the cold, carbonated, caffeinated liquid surge into her system. After several more swallows which finished the can, she felt almost ready to face Matthew and what she was certain would be the continuation of their "discussion" from the night before.

Stay strong, stay calm, stay in control. Do not let him bulldoze you. North Carolina is a right to work state and you have every right to hold a job.

But Matthew was late for work. He did not have time to comment on the events of the previous evening. Instead of continuing that discussion, he poured his coffee into a travel mug while again blaming her for his oversleeping. Nothing was said of her job or that he expected her to quit. Had he forgotten? Or did he take it for granted that she would do as he decreed?

It was only after he drove away that she took a relaxed breath. Then and only then did she focus on her day. Though JJ had given her the morning off, she planned to be there at nine, just like always.

She walked into the office at 8:55 and was surprised to find both bosses sitting in the conference room listening to a third man make some kind of a presentation. After one look at JJ who nodded her way, she went to the kitchen and put on a fresh pot of coffee. Whatever was going on, they appeared to be only half awake.

When she had left hours before, they had not talked about stopping their work on the house any time soon. She could only assume they finished the clean up before calling it a night. So they had slept even less than she had.

A half-hour after delivering an insulated carafe of fresh coffee to the conference room, the meeting broke up. As he walked out, the third man assured Cody and JJ that he would return before noon with everything set up as they requested. JJ came in only long enough to grab the briefcase. Then he followed the man out of the building.

Cody entered a few minutes later, an envelope in one hand. He laid it on the desk beside her elbow, then took a seat across the desk. "I want you to take this," he said.

"What is it?" she asked, as she picked it up.

"Open it and see."

The flap had not been sealed, so she pulled it open and looked inside. There was a stack of green papers with printing on them. It took a moment to register that she was looking at a lot of money. Thumbing through it revealed they were hundred dollar bills. Several thousand dollars worth if she had to make a guess.

"What's this?" she asked as she laid the envelope back her desk.

"Five thousand dollars," Cody said as if that explained everything.

"Why?"

"So you can leave that SOB and start over. Is it enough?" he asked. He sounded like he would pull more money out of his ear if she said it wasn't.

She looked from him back to the envelope. She blinked back

tears as she smiled a sad smile. Swallowing hard, she tucked the flap back around the money. In the hardest act she had ever performed, she extended her arm and held the envelope out to him.

"Thanks, but I can't take this," she said.

"Why not?" he asked, stunned by her refusal.

"I don't want your charity. I can't start my new life owing you thousands of dollars. Who knows when I'd ever be able to pay it all back? Besides, you need this money to renovate that bathroom upstairs." She laid the envelope on the desk, then slid it toward him.

Cody looked like he wanted to argue, but when he opened his mouth, a yawn caught him by surprise. "I'll let it go for now, but if you ever need it..." he let the rest of the offer unsaid.

Her smile widened. "Thanks Boss, but I got myself into this and now I have to get myself out."

"Yeah, well. That guy who just left is going to be dropping off three new cell phones. JJ and I want you to take one of them. Keep it with you and charged, just in case you need it. Don't be afraid of using it to make personal calls." When she opened her mouth to argue, he frowned at her. "Consider it part of your new uniform. A third line did not cost anything extra and when you start hunting with us you'll need it."

She nodded. "Thanks."

"You know, if you won't take money from me, have you thought about asking your family? Or demand your husband give you money? If he's in charge of all the money, you deserve half, at least." Cody made then statement, then yawned again. "I'm going upstairs."

"Yes, sir," she said, throwing him a two-fingered salute.

After he left the room she sat, stunned by Cody's last words. He was right. What Matthew had squirreled away over their years together did belong to both of them. She had supported him for ten years so he could earn it. She was entitled to half of whatever was in their bank accounts.

All at once her heart was pounding too fast and too hard. Escape was within her grasp. All she had to do was go to the bank, withdraw half of what was in their accounts and leave. But then what?

She couldn't withdraw the money until she was ready to walk out the door. She needed to know how much she could take so she could make plans, but she couldn't take the money until she was ready to leave. Otherwise Matthew would wonder what the hell she was doing. And right now she was nowhere near ready. She had no where to go.

Her giddy excitement stalled, fear of the unknown taking its place. Could it really be this simple? Did it really come down to packing her bags and making a withdrawal at the bank? There had to be more to it. It could not be that simple.

Before she got too caught up in what her next move should be, she needed some information. Looking up Matthew's bank in the phone book, she called the toll free number listed. She listened to all the options, but none of them fit what she needed. When she did not make a selection, the telephone auto-responder finally put her through to a live person.

Two minutes later after verifying six different pieces of information, the clerk pulled up their accounts and read the numbers. She was stunned to hear there was less than a thousand dollars in the savings and checking accounts combined. She thanked the woman and hung up, staring at the numbers she'd written down.

Matthew made a very good income, or so he claimed. Where did it all go? She had a rough idea of what their bills were and Matthew kept telling her he was receiving raises and bonuses. So what happened to all that money?

For the next two hours, she brooded and wondered and came to the realization that Matthew had been lying to her, probably for years. Then she got angry. First at Matthew for lying about so many things and then at herself for being so meek that she did not question what was going on around her.

What would happen if he dropped dead tomorrow? She knew nothing except which bank their checking and savings accounts were in. Did they have insurance? Would if cover the costs of a funeral and the mortgage and the other bills? Was Matthew hiding money from her for reasons only he would understand?

Should she take Cody up on his offer of money to start her new life? That was the question that bamboozled her the most because she was tempted to do it.

Chapter 14

By the time she left the office for the day, she understood the basics of her brand new cell phone and had even learned how to save phone numbers into the memory. The first three she entered into the speed dial were the main office number, JJ and Cody. Then she added Nikki's home and office numbers and her mother. After that she had no one else to add. She never called Matthew at work.

That was another of the unwritten, unspoken rules of their marriage. When they were dating, Matthew often called during his lunch hour or in the middle of the afternoon. He usually chose times when she was busy with her own work. Once they were married, the phone calls dwindled until he only called if he would be late for dinner. Then even those stopped.

She called a couple of times during the first years of their marriage, but stopped when he told her flat out one day that unless it was an emergency, she should wait until he got home. He went on to point out that while he loved her, he needed to focus on his job so he did not get fired. That evening he apologized for being curt with her by bringing her two dozen roses. She had been tempted on occasion, but she had never again called him at work.

As soon as she arrived home, she did a few deep-breathing exercises to calm her nerves then hit the speed dial on the cell phone to connect with her mother. This would be one of the hardest conversations of her life, but Cody was right. It was past time to get out of her marriage. But she did not want to have to take his money. She would ask Nikki, but her friend had just bought a new house and was up to her eyeballs with mortgage payments herself.

"Hello?" Her mother answered on the second ring.

"Hi Mom." She forced the corners of her mouth into a semblance of a smile. But the phone trick did not fool her mother.

"Hi honey, what's wrong?"

"How do you know something's wrong?"

"You're calling me. It's not my birthday or a holiday. What's wrong?"

Taking a deep breath and closing her eyes, she paced the kitchen as she said, "I'm planning to leave Matthew and get a divorce." She went on to fill her mother in on the secrets she had been keeping for the last years.

"So why haven't you left him already?" her mother asked, not sounding at all surprised by the announcement

"Because I have no money. I was wondering if you could loan me a couple of thousand dollars?" she asked before she lost what little nerve she still had. Asking the question proved harder than she ever imagined.

Her mother was silent for such a long time that she began to wonder if the connection had been lost. Finally her mother said, "Honey, I'd love to give you the money you need, but you know your father. Marriage is marriage and you have got to sleep in the bed you made. He would never allow me to give you that much money, no matter what the reason. But I'm here if you need to talk. I have to go now. There's someone at the door." Her mother hung up before she could react.

"Bye Mom," she said to the dial tone.

Blinking back tears of frustration, she hung up the phone, then checked to make sure the ring tone was on meeting. It would beep if she got a message, but would otherwise be silent. She slid the slim phone into one of the inside pockets of her purse. The charger was at work so Matthew would not know about it. She felt sneaky and dishonest about the preparations she was putting in place. She knew everything would work out sooner or later. It had to.

In the meantime, she was on her own and had to maintain the status quo while she earned her escape fund. Tomorrow she would use the office computer to research what exactly was involved in becoming a licensed bail enforcement agent. Then she would work on the next step in her professional development.

For the next weeks she walked the fine line of balancing work, training and home life. She added a basic workout of calisthenics, walking and slow jogging, hoping to lose weight and get in shape. She also began to diet a thing she tried in the past, but had never stuck with for long.

"Eat something," Matthew insisted one night about a week after she grown super-serious about her diet and exercise routine.

"I am. I'm eating a salad, see?" She pointed to the bowl in front of her.

It was a basic lettuce salad with green peppers, tomatoes and cucumbers, the same as the salad that sat untouched next to his plate. The only difference was that hers also had a sprinkle of sliced almonds and shredded cheese as well as one hard-boiled egg while he had a full plate of meatloaf, mashed potatoes and green beans.

"That's not a suitable dinner. You need to eat some real food, meat and potatoes. I'll get you a plate," Matthew rose and left the dining room before she could argue further.

For the next five minutes she fought a losing battle, finally giving in to his grandmother-like nagging. She filled her plate with meatloaf and mashed potatoes, then proceeded to eat every bite. Only when she was washing dishes a few minutes later did she kick herself. Her stomach was so full it hurt and though she felt sick, she could not make herself throw up the food she had not wanted, but had eaten anyway.

In her mind, she rehearsed the words she should have said to Matthew. "You need to make up your mind. Do you want me to lose weight or do you want me to eat dinner with you each night?"

She knew he would hem and haw and somehow lay it all back on her. He was starting to watch her as if she has grown a second head or something. So far nothing further had been said about her job, but she remained vigilant and hyperaware that she had to keep up with her chores as she always had.

Life with Matthew was not great, but it was familiar, comfortable. It was what she knew. The world she envisioned on her own was...she could not imagine life on her own after ten years of marriage. She had been serving Matthew for so long she was not sure she could make it alone.

With every paycheck he handed her, Cody asked the same question, "Need that loan yet?"

She would just shake her head. "Not yet, thanks, but I'll keep you in mind."

After she was able to jog a mile at a good clip without stopping for a rest or gasping for breath at the end, she found that Craven Community College offered the class she needed to get her BEA license. She offered several times to help with tracking a bail jumper, but Cody refused each time. "Not until your license is hanging on the conference room wall." He also decided she needed a handgun permit and permit to carry a concealed weapon. She felt that a Taser and a can of pepper spray would be more than enough defense against the kind of criminals they went after, but he was adamant. Since he was the boss, she agreed to attend a class offered by the local gun club.

* * * * *

It took another six weeks, but she earned the license to be a bail enforcement agent. The day she received the certificate and paperwork in the mail, she stopped at Target on her way home and bought a frame. The next morning she hung the frame in the conference room just below JJ's. Her hammering brought JJ into the room.

"Way to go," he said, patting her shoulder. "You know that now we'll be calling you when we need a third man for a job."

"Yes, sir," she said, throwing him a two-fingered salute that was respectful, yet sassy, at the same time.

* * * * *

"Mom and Dad's anniversary is next week," Matthew said during dinner that evening.

"I bought them a card already," she said as she spooned green beans onto her plate.

"It's been awhile since we've seen them," he continued as if she hadn't spoken, "so I invited them to come to dinner that evening. I thought you could make a roast and bake that pineapple cake Dad likes so much."

"Uh huh," she said. Instead of running for a notebook to make a list of chores to accomplish and foods to buy at the grocery store, she added another spoonful of beans to her plate.

With each accomplishment at work her backbone strengthened. But each conversation like this caused it to weakening a bit. Forcing herself to eat, she wondered if she would ever be strong enough to break free of Matthew.

* * * * *

Two nights later that same thought crossed her mind. It was Saturday night and she had not heard Matthew's return after his evening out with the boys. Disoriented, she woke to find a hot, sweaty hand was groping between her thighs. The self-defense classes she was taking kicked in. She grabbed the wrist attached to the hand and pulled it away from her body and out from under the covers. “No,” she said.

Chapter 15

"What?" Matthew asked, somehow managing to spit in her eye as she frowned up at him.

"No," she said, rolling away.

"Whaddaya mean no? You're my wife. You can't say no," Matthew said, reaching to pull her back into the bed.

Before he could touch her she rolled out of bed, beyond of his reach. "Yes, I can tell you no. I am an American citizen, free and over twenty-one, not some blow-up Playboy bunny doll here for your amusement." She took a few seconds to straighten her nightshirt from where it was twisted around her waist but stood firm.

"I know you're not a blow up doll, but since you've been working out you're starting to look like the woman I married. It's been awhile since we've done it and I feel the horns breaking through."

He'd left the bathroom light so the room was just bright enough to see he had shifted to lay on his side. He was giving her what he thought was a come-hither look while rubbing his palm over the top of his head. It was his way of a joking that he was so in need of sex that goat horns were beginning to grow and would soon break through the skin.

She had never found this so-called joke funny, but never more so than tonight. "You're right, it has been awhile. But I'm tired of you having to go out and drink too many beers to get in the mood. The next time you wake me up by groping me like that, I'll break a finger or two." She swallowed hard and breathed deep to keep tears of intense anger from springing forth.

Stay in control. Do not let him see you weaken or you will lose this round.

"I don't know what the hell's gotten into you lately," Matthew grumbled as he rolled over to his side of the bed. "All I wanted to do was show you that I approve of the new you and you get all bitchy on me. Are you on the ra..." his voice trailed off and he was snoring before he finished asking the question.

"No, I'm not on the rag," she said. "I've just grown some long overdue self-esteem." She grabbed her pillow from the bed and walked out of the room without another glance.

She spent the rest of the night curled up on the guest bed under the wedding ring quilt her grandmother had given them. She did not sleep; her mind was too wound up. Every time she closed her eyes, she began listing the things she wanted to finish before she could move out. Some were old things, some were new, but because her mind was racing she could not sleep.

Turning on the bedside light, she crawled from under the quilt and went to the kitchen. After drinking a glass of milk to ease the gnawing in her belly, she pulled the notebook and a pen out of the very bottom of her purse and returned to the guestroom.

She had not looked at the notes she had made in months. It was time to reread them and reevaluate what she really needed to do before she packed her bags and left. She had nearly three thousand dollars in the bank. If she found a cheap apartment, she might be able to get her new life started now. She would get a second job if she had to, but she had to leave and soon. It was getting harder and harder to hold back her feelings of revulsion and the comments she wanted to spear Matthew with, but she was trying to keep things civil.

When dawn brightened the skyline outside the guestroom window, she was ready to take the next step in reclaiming herself. It was Sunday morning and she was going to church. For most of their marriage, Matthew refused to go to church except on special occasions. Christenings, weddings and funerals were the only time he darkened the church's door. Easter and Christmas were a toss up, depending on his mood. Just an ordinary Sunday morning was not a good enough reason to wake up early, put on a suit and go to services.

Whenever she tried to talk him into going with her, he always said, "My relationship with God is my business. I don't need anyone else telling me how I'm supposed to behave."

He gave her such a hard time about it that she stopped attending Sunday services as well. It was easier not to go alone than to go through the inquisition he put her through every time she went out without him. He demanded a minute by minute accounting of where she went, the names of everyone she spoke to, what was said and why she felt the need to go. In the case of church, he also wanted to know why she let someone else tell her how to live.

On those rare Sundays she attended services, she arrived as the call to worship was playing and tried to slip out during the last hymn. She sat in the back row and tried not to speak to anyone. On her way home she usually stopped at Wal-Mart to pick up a bag of donuts and a broasted chicken fresh from the rotisserie.

If she were able to wake up early enough to attend the eight o'clock service, she would return before Matthew woke up. If she was lucky, she could change her clothes before he was fully conscious. If not, the questions began and continued until he felt he knew her every move.

This morning she needed the emotional and spiritual comfort only an hour in God's house could provide her with. Whether or not she answered Matthew's questions when she returned was something she would think about later. For now, she was going to church.

She took a quick shower, then blew her hair dry, put on makeup, dressed and headed out. There was still an hour and half before the early service began, but she left the house anyway. If she had to, she would sit in the church's parking lot, but she had to get away from the house and the man who controlled her self worth with the crook of an eyebrow or offhand comment. The anger that had erupted in the early morning hours when Matthew had molested her while she'd been sleeping had yet to cool. If anything, its heat and intensity had grown.

But it was not just Matthew that fired her anger. It was also disgust with herself and her actions or lack thereof. While the last months had been profitable and a true period of physical growth she had remained apathetic in following through on her plans to leave.

Instead of driving straight to the church, she drove to IHOP. The parking lot was only half full so she pulled in. Before she climbed from the car though, she opened her wallet to make sure she had enough money to pay for breakfast and still have money for the offering plate at church. Twelve dollars and a handful of change. She should be able to eat a great breakfast on that.

An hour later she felt almost optimistic as she pulled into the church parking lot. Pancakes with blueberry syrup, bacon and hot chocolate had something to do with the improvement in her mood. Not having to cook the meal had more to do with it. Over the last years, it was the little things, like super crisp bacon and fluffy whip cream on her hot chocolate that caused her to smile.

She was tempted to scrunch down in the seat of her car and hide until 7:58. She could watch the crowd go into church, then join them at the last second as she always had. That option was taken out of her hands with a sharp tap at her window. She turned and her expression of fear turned to a smile of greeting. Henrietta Simmons was smiling and waving at her. With a nod and a motion to come out, the old woman stepped back and readjusted her grip on her silver-headed cane. Feeling trapped yet relieved, she climbed from the car, locked it and made sure she had her keys in her hand before she pushed the door closed.

As soon as her feet hit the pavement, Henrietta started talking, asking questions and sharing news of the various members of the library newsletter committee then had both served on. She smiled and made appropriate noises, while trying not to answer the questions thrown at her.

Henrietta stayed by her side as they entered the church. Once inside the elderly woman took her arm and guided her toward the pew in the middle of the church where she and her friends sat. "You'll sit with us today. You have friends Child, no matter what your husband tells you."

She wanted to ask what the elderly woman meant, but just then Reverend Powell walked through the church, greeting members and checking to make sure everything was ready for services. When he saw her, he stopped, his smile broadened and he headed in their direction. "It's so good to see you this morning," he said giving her a long hug filled with Christian warmth.

She blinked back tears and returned the hug, "Thank you," she whispered.

"God bless you. If you need anything just ask," he murmured before releasing her.

His words caused her tears to press harder behind her eyelids. She blinked several times to control them before they could spill out. Her smile was shaky, but it was a genuine smile and felt very right. Matthew was wrong. She did need church. For the friendships, the love and the acceptance as well as to worship her God.

During the next hour, she soaked up the calm, the fellowship and the holiness of the sanctuary. It had been months since she'd attended a service and she had missed it. She felt like a sponge dunked into a bucket of warm water after a long, long dry spell. She recognized the hymns and identified with the sermon on allowing God to take your worry and deal with it. Several times she had to wipe tears from her cheeks. She could not explain why they flowed, but as they leaked from her eyes, she felt her anger and frustration at Matthew lighten. By the end of the service, she was praying for guidance, for forgiveness, for a shove in the right direction when it came to her marriage, her job and her life.

She could not escape during the last hymn as she usually did. Henrietta had taken her hand and would not let go. So she waited. The benediction entered her heart, adding another layer of peace to her soul. She joined those around her in a final Amen before picking up her purse and slowly working her way to the back of the church with the rest of the congregation. Reverend Powell hugged her again just outside the church doors, again blessing her. She blinked back tears and headed to her car, afraid to speak to anyone for fear of having an emotional meltdown and refusing to leave this place that had given her such peace.

Chapter 16

By Wednesday she had begun to dread agreeing to the anniversary dinner for Matthew's parents. He had been grumpy as a bear since waking late Sunday morning, picking at everything she did or said. She was afraid of what he might say in front of his parents. He sniped and picked and criticized about everything from the amount of sugar in the iced tea to the black slacks and ivory blouse she intended to wear. She should not have worried.

As soon as he opened the door for his parents though, he blinked and it was as if a switch had been flipped in his personality. He was cheerful and helpful and complimentary. Most of his backhanded compliments were delivered in a sharp-edged tone, but his parents did not catch on. They acted as if nothing was any different than any of their other visits. And that was the truth. Matthew always complimented her in a way that felt like he was stabbing her with the roses he offered.

No one else realized his kind words flailed at her until her ego and nerves were raw from trying not to lash back. She forced herself to keep smiling, keep acting, keep up the façade of a happy couple. It would only be for a few hours. Then she could retreat to the bathroom and cry after their guests were gone.

No one noticed the slight bulge in her pocket. The weight of the small cell phone was new to her and she kept putting her hand in her pocket to remind herself of what she carried there.

Before she left work that afternoon, she had changed the ring tone so it vibrated silently. JJ told her that afternoon to keep her phone with her. They were going after a husband and wife team who'd failed to appear in court and they might need her to escort the wife back to jail. When the phone jumped and buzzed against her leg in the middle of dinner, she leapt out of her chair like someone had touched her with a cattle prod.

She rushed from the dining room without a word to the three people who were staring at her. She didn't answer Matthew's "Are you all right?" as she stepped into the half bath and closed the door. Once inside she pulled the phone out of her pocket and flipped it open.

"Hello?"

"We need you," JJ said without preamble. He rattled of the address, and then reminded her to bring the special bag they'd put together.

"I'll be there in ten minutes," she said, allowing a few minutes to extricate herself from the house.

"Five would be better," JJ said before hanging up.

She closed and repocketed the phone before opening the bathroom door.

Matthew was standing just outside looking like a thundercloud, dark and ominous. "Are you all right?" he asked, his voice deceptively soft and venomous.

"I'm fine, but I have to go out for a little bit."

"Go out? Where are you going? My parents are in there wondering if its safe to finish eating their dinner."

"Don't worry, dinner is fine. I just have an errand to run." Before he could stop her, she had stepped around him and headed for the front door. Her equipment bag was already in her car, but she needed the black sweatshirt from the closet. Once she had slipped it on, she turned and headed to the kitchen.

"What errand? Where are you going? Is it another man? It is, isn't it?" Matthew continued questioning her in a furious whisper as he followed her through to the kitchen.

He had been stomping on her last nerve all week. All at once she had had enough. "No, Matthew, it's not one man. It's two. I'm going to meet two men. Then we're going to meet another couple and get into it." The truth, but one he would take entirely wrong.

Her words shocked him so much that he froze in the kitchen doorway, unable to speak. She stepped into her new black sneakers, grabbed her purse and left without further interference. She was pulling out of the driveway when he appeared beside her car. She could just make out his words through the car window. "I'm sick of your shit. If you don't come back inside right now, don't bother coming home."

She waved and drove away.

The address JJ had given her was halfway across town. By driving well over the speed limit and praying for a clear path, she made the drive in less than the five minutes JJ had requested. As she drove, she reached toward the floor just behind the passenger's seat. She felt for, then held the strap and dragged the oversized black nylon sports bag into the front seat with her. Anyone who looked in the back seat would think it was a gym bag, not a bag full of equipment for the professional bounty hunter she was in training to be.

JJ was beside the car before she had pulled the keys from the ignition. "That was fast," he said as he opened the door for her.

"You said five minutes. It's been seven," she said, stuffing her purse under the driver's seat and pulling the bag out of the car with her.

"Yeah, but I expected you in fifteen," he said, taking the bag from her.

"Uh huh," she followed him to the SUV where Cody waited.

* * * * *

The next hour was one of the most intense and eye opening of her life. While Cody and JJ went around to the back of the house, she went to the front door and rang the bell. With luck, Frannie and Bobby Joe Southerland would let her in, cooperate and she would have them loaded in the SUV and on their way to jail in just a few minutes. That was her prayer. But just in case plan A failed, JJ and Cody were armed to the teeth and waiting.

Frannie Southerland opened the door several long minutes after she rang the doorbell. "Yeah, whaddaya want?" the woman asked, blowing smoke as she talked.

Frannie was a human fireplug; five feet tall and two hundred pounds according to her file. She had answered the door at seven o'clock in the evening wearing a skintight blood red camisole and a pair of tiny leopard print panties that barely held her in. She couldn't be sure, but she suspected it was a thong. The deep tan that appeared to be full body emphasized the leathery skin and wrinkles she had developed over the years. Her peroxide blonde hair with an inch of black roots did not help soften her appearance. She looked much older than the mid-forties the file reported her to be.

"Well?" Frannie crossed her arms after taking another puff on her cigarette.

"Ma'am, I work for C&JJ Bail Bonds and you missed your court date this morning. We need to go down to the courthouse..."

She was only partway through her speech when Frannie swore. The woman threw her cigarette past her into the tall grass of the yard, then pulled one flabby arm up and back. "Bobby Joe, get your lazy ass outta bed. They've come to take us in." With that, the pudgy fingers folded into a fist and she swung.

At the same moment a male voice called, "What?" a crash

sounded from the back of the trailer.

She was not prepared for the fist that came flying her way. All her self-defense training went out the window. Frannie's fist caught her just under her left eye. The blow knocked her off the small cement stoop and she hit the ground on palms and knees. She heard a snap at the same time she felt it as her left wrist took the brunt of her weight.

Pain rocketed through her from face and wrist. She sunk into a dark haze for a few seconds. She could not pass out now. She was a bail enforcement agent, dammit, and her quarry was heading across the overgrown yard. As Frannie waddled away, she was struggling to pull on a pair of glittery silver stretch pants she had grabbed from somewhere.

Gritting her teeth against the throbbing pain in her arm, she struggled to her feet and started after Frannie. Yep, the woman was wearing a thong and it was not a pretty sight from here.

She tried a technique her self-defense instructor had talked about. She turned her pain into anger. Dashing across the yard, she reached Frannie just as the other woman reached an old red pickup truck. Without a word, she grabbed for Frannie's shoulder length braid and pulled. At the same time she screamed. "JJ, HELP!" She managed to pull Frannie back two steps from the truck before the other woman stopped and turned on her.

"OWWWW! You bitch, let me go!"

The anger blazing in Frannie's eyes caused her to release the braid and step back, hoping she was out of range. For a moment she wondered if she would survive another attack if Frannie got mad at her. Anger still heated her blood, but the pain was pulsing through it, making her lightheaded.

"Use the taser," a deep voice ordered from behind her.

Oh yeah, since I'm wearing all these cool bounty hunter toys, why don't I use one or two of them?

She fumbled at her utility belt for the taser while stepping back, trying to stay just out of Frannie's reach. Flipping the on switch at the base of the handset, she did not wait the five seconds for the taser to charge. She pointed it at the bull of a woman charging at her and pushed the discharge button. But nothing happened.

Before she could figure out what went wrong, Frannie knocked the arm holding the taser to the side out of her way and then slammed a fist into the right side of her jaw. As she hit the ground, she did remembered to roll to soften the landing.

As she finished a backward somersault, Cody arrived to body slam Frannie to the ground. With ease of practice, he flipped the stout woman on her belly and straddled her. She watched through a haze of pain as he caught one arm and then the other, securing them together with a nylon zipcord. His biggest challenge was to maintain his balance as Frannie bucked and rolled, trying to throw him off. The whole time she was cursing at the top of her lungs and screaming for Bobby Joe to come and help her.

Once her hands were secure, Cody pulled a second cord and immobilized her feet. Frannie continued fussing and cussing until he rolled her onto her back, bent over and got right in her face. "Shut up or I'll gag you," he growled in a tone that got her attention.

In response, she spit at him.

"That's it," he said, reaching into his pocket and pulling out a green bandana. He rolled it into a long tube, then forced the makeshift rope between her lips and tied it behind her head.

Finally the woman was still and quiet, chest heaving as she caught her breath. Cody left Frannie on the ground and turned to her.

"You okay?" He came over and offered a hand. She took it with her right hand and pulled herself to her feet. As soon as she was upright, he let go, but grabbed her when she swayed and her knees buckled. "Nope, you're not okay. Okay, let's go sit you down," he wrapped an arm around her and half carried her to their SUV. Opening the front passenger door, he lifted her and set her on the seat. He disappeared for a few seconds, then returned to place an ice pack against the right side of her face.

"Hold that there. It will help with the swelling."

She nodded, making a face when the slight movement hurt.

"Stay here," he ordered before disappearing again. She turned her head and watched as he and JJ lifted Frannie between them and carried her to the SUV. They hefted her into the trunk. Bobby Joe was shoved in next to her and the trunk door closed. JJ climbed into the backseat and Cody drove.

No one spoke on the way to the courthouse. The only sound was Bobby Joe's snoring and Frannie's grunts as they drove over a set of railroad tracks. Once they dropped the prisoners off and did the paperwork, they drove back to her car.

She was lost in a foggy world of pain, fighting to keep from crying as they drove. When Cody parked behind her car, she struggled to unbuckle her seatbelt.

"Where do you think you're going?" he asked as he pulled her hand away from the seatbelt release.

"Home," she said.

"Not like this. You need to see a doctor. Give JJ your keys and he'll follow us." He looked like he was going to hog-tie her if she did not cooperate.

Taking a deep breath, she pulled her key ring out of her front right pocket and handed them over. "I need to go home. Matthew was very upset I left during dinner. I need to get back."

"You need to get checked out by a doctor. Don't worry, the company will be covering this," Cody put the car in gear as soon as JJ climbed out and closed the back door. He drove slowly until JJ caught up. Then in a two-car caravan, they headed to the hospital.

Chapter 17

"So, how did this happen?" Dr. Williams, the emergency room physician, asked in a gentle tone. He did not look at her. He was busy examining the x-ray clipped to the light box.

"I was trying apprehend a bail jumper and she knocked me off the porch. I landed on my arm."

"Uh huh," the doctor said. He did not believe her, even though it was the truth. He turned and looked at the bruises coloring the side of her face. "Are you going to press charges?"

"We already have," Cody answered from the doorway. He looked at her and frowned. "You want me to call your husband?"

"NO!" she cried. Her eyes went wide, but she bit the inside of her cheek to keep from saying anything else. Both men frowned at her, but she shook her head. Matthew did not need to know about this. Not yet. Morning would be soon enough.

Dr. Williams looked at Cody who shrugged, but did not argue. The doctor turned to face her. "I have called the on-call orthopedic doctor. He should be here soon. Do you want something for the pain in the meantime?"

She shook her head slowly. "I've done okay so far," she said through gritted teeth.

"Sir, you must go back to the waiting room," a nurse said, pushing Cody out of the doorway so she could enter the room. "You are scaring the other patients and making the staff nervous."

Cody looked at her and smiled though his expression was wolfish and dangerous. "I'm scaring them? I'm a pussycat," he said, stepping so he was just inside the room, leaning against the wall, as out of the way as he could manage while still being there.

"Nevertheless you are not family and will have to wait out front," the petite nurse in navy blue scrubs squared off with him, planting her hands on her hips. "If I have to I will call security."

"That's really not necessary. Go on out Cody," she said.

"You gonna be okay?" He ignored the nurse and looked at the patient with a skeptical expression.

"I'll be fine. Go on. I'll be out soon."

Cody stared into her eyes for another minute before giving up. He shrugged again and stalked away. The nurse followed him every step of the way back to the waiting room.

An hour and a half later, she was finally released. The orthopedic doctor arrived, questioned her again about how her injuries occurred before confirming a hairline fracture at her left wrist. After putting a plain white cast on her arm, the nurse handed her a vial of painkillers and information sheets on taking care of her arm and her bruised face. The orthopedic doctor also instructed her to make an appointment in a week with his office so they could make sure the bone was healing properly.

She returned to the waiting room to find JJ and Cody prowling the room like jungle cats in a room full of tabbies. When she stepped through the doorway everyone else in the room looked relieved. The men rushed to her side, each carefully taking an elbow.

"What did the doctor say?" JJ asked.

"Cracked humerus, otherwise just a collection of bumps and

bruises," she said, wincing as the skin pulled around her mouth. "Nothing that should keep me out of work."

Neither man laughed at her sad attempt at humor.

Ten minutes later JJ parked her car in the driveway of her house and helped her out of the SUV. He handed her the keys to her car before climbing into the passenger's seat she just climbed out of.

"You sure about this?" he asked as she hitched her purse more securely over her shoulder.

"Matthew probably won't even realize I've come home. He's been asleep for hours and won't wake up until his alarm goes off in the morning. I'll be fine. I'll see you at the office at nine."

"Don't come in if you're hurting too much. And if he gives you any trouble, call us and we'll come get you," Cody said, his voice gruff. He did not look at all happy. She was not sure what he wanted, but knew he did not want to drive away.

"I'll see you in the morning," she said forcing herself to smile.

She turned and headed inside, surprised to find a light glowing softly in the living room windows. Matthew never left a light on for her. It was not his way, though she had never tested the theory by staying out late at night. In fact, she rarely went out after the sun went down. What was going on?

As was her habit, she went to the back door. It was unlocked, which was another surprise. Matthew always locked the house up tight before he went to bed.

She was toeing her sneakers off in the kitchen when the overhead light flashed on. She flinched at the sudden brightness, then winced as the movement of her face caused pain to shaft through the bruised side of her face.

"Where the hell have you been?"

"Working," she answered, too tired and in too much pain to be clever. She turned around and he stared at her as if she'd suddenly turned green. Only she wasn't green, she was black and blue with touches of purple. Or at least half of her face was. The other half was still pale ivory skin.

"What the hell happened to you?"

"I had a run in with an angry fireplug."

"Why are you here? I told you that if you left you were not welcome back," He enunciated each syllable, a sure sign that he had been drinking in her absence. He stood in the doorway to the living room, arms crossed, looking like a banty rooster with his stringy legs and body covered only in a pair of silky turquoise boxer shorts with fluorescent orange smiley faces on them.

"I'm tired, I hurt and it's late. I want to go to bed," she said, toeing off her other sneaker.

"You are not sleeping here tonight. You are no longer welcome in this house. I don't know what has happened to you the last couple of months, but I don't know who you are any more. Put your shoes back on and get out."

She stared at him for a long moment. He was serious. He did not want her here. Though it was sudden, this was just the impetus she needed to start her new life. For a moment she saw herself at the edge of the cliff like the one the cartoon coyote was always falling off. She was holding a pair of almost finished wings in her hands. The wings she had spent the last few months building. Matthew had just shoved her off the cliff and she was standing in mid air, waiting to fall and become a grease spot on the canyon floor. Only she was not going to become a grease spot. She was going to finish building her wings on the way down and soar away before she crashed.

Taking a deep breath, she nodded. She slipped her shoes back on, picked up her purse and walked out. She did not think. All she could do was marvel at the stunned, weightless feeling that encompassed her. Like she really was flying. She climbed in her car and drove away. Halfway across town she stopped for a red light and the reality of the last few minutes hit her like a hand upside the back of her head.

Matthew had kicked her out.

She was on her own.

It was time to fly.

"Oh my God," she moaned as tears pushed against the back of her eyes. "I'm homeless without a change of clothes or grandmother's quilt."

For a moment she panicked. What did she do now? She had nowhere to go. She only had about forty dollars in her wallet. She was not sure if Matthew had closed her charge accounts, but she was not willing to embarrass herself by trying to rent a motel room just to have her card declined or taken away from her and cut up.

The light turned green, then red again and still she sat there. Halfway through this light cycle, a car pulled to a stop behind her. Its lights reflected in her rear view mirror, blinding her. This time when the light changed, she drove with no destination in mind. She headed to the shopping strip. She needed clean clothes that were not covered in dirt and grass stains. It was two o'clock in the morning and the only place she knew that would be open was Wal-Mart.

Twenty minutes later she walked out of Wal-Mart wearing brand new blue jeans and a red T-shirt. She carried one bag holding her old clothes and a second that held fruit and a box of granola bars and two bottles of water. As she crossed to her car she watched a giant RV pull into the parking lot and head to an area well away from the building. The big rig parked and then a man appeared and seemed to be doing something to the wheels. That's when she remembered an article she'd read once about how Wal-Mart allowed campers to park in their lots overnight rent free.

"If it works for them, it should work for me," she murmured.

She gave no thought about going to the battered women's shelter. That was for women whose husbands beat them or threatened their lives. Her husband had never physically hurt her, he had just thrown her out of their house.

She pulled in between two RVs, trying not to park too close to either of them. After putting the keys in her pocket, she wiggled over the center console and gearshift to the passenger's seat.

Once there, she lay the back down as far as she could and tried to get comfortable.

She took a deep breath and relaxed. Tears began to roll down her cheeks in rapid succession. Physical pain was eclipsed by the emotional agony. Resentment, anger, fear and uncertainty had been boxed up in the small place near her heart, refused to stay caged any longer. Emotions swelled, broke their bonds and rolled over her like an avalanche of sadness.

Turning on her side, she curled her knees to her chest and sobbed. She had held this back for so long that she could control the pain no longer. When her nose began to run and her shirt grew damp from tears, she reached into the back seat and grabbed the black sweatshirt she had worn earlier. She pulled it over the seat and held it to her face, hiding from the world.

She cried until her head was stopped up, her right eye was almost as swollen as her left and her head thrummed steadily with pain. Finally the tears stopped. She dried her face and blew her nose into the shirt. Then she began to hiccup as she did every time she cried hard like this.

Once the emotional tsunami subsided, she relaxed. She sniffed and hiccuped for a few more minutes until sleep crept up from around her toes and covered her like a soft fleece blanket. She gave no thought to the future. She gave no thought to the past. She just enjoyed the return of the weightless feeling of freedom.

* * * * *

Bang. Bang. Bang. The sharp sounds jerked her from sleep, her heart pounding in her throat. She uncurled on the seat and looked around. For a moment she was lost. Why was she sleeping in her car? Then she remembered the last hours. Matthew had kicked her out and she had nowhere else to go.

The knock came at the window just behind her head and she shifted in her seat. A flashlight blinded her as she reached for the handle that would manually roll down the window. Thankfully she had thought enough to lock the doors. She lowered the window two inches with one hand while the one in the cast was raised to block the intense light that still blinded her.

"Yes?" she asked when the person on the other side of the door remained silent.

"Is everything all right, ma'am?" A deep voice asked.

"Yes, thank you," she said, all at once nervous that things might not be as all right as she wanted him to believe.

"Could I see your driver's license and registration?" Finally the man lowered the flashlight and aimed it at her lap instead of her face.

"Why? Is something wrong?" she asked as she reached for her purse.

"There was some concern that you might be having car trouble. Are you?"

"No. I..." She paused, not sure how to explain that she had to spend the night here because she had been kicked out of her home and did not have the money for a motel room.

"Yes?" The officer sounded even more wary when she paused.

"My husband kicked me out and I don't have anywhere to go. I don't have much money so I can't get a motel room. When I saw these campers parked out here, I figured no one would mind if I stayed here tonight, too."

"Did he give you that black eye?" the officer asked.

"No, I got that from my job." She dropped her chin and concentrated on getting her license from her wallet. Then she pulled the car registration from the holder over the visor. Holding both out through the crack in the window, she waited while the officer inspected them.

"I'm sorry, but you can't sleep here. You'll have to either go to a motel or..." he paused as he handed her documents back.

"Or?" she asked, already dreading the alternative.

"You could go home and apologize to your husband. Or are you afraid he might hurt you?" Clearly he did not believe that she had earned the black eye at work. He was trying to figure out if Matthew would beat her if she returned home.

"No, he won't beat me. He kicked me out. I can't go home. I'm never going back there," she said, her words a vow to herself more than to the policeman.

"Well, you can't stay here. You have to leave. Now." The officer's statement was made in a flat tone that allowed her no room for argument.

She sighed and nodded. "Yes, sir," she said.

Taking her keys, she climbed out of the passenger seat, circled the front of the car and climbed into the driver's seat. The police officer waited until she started her car before turning toward his cruiser.

She pulled out of the parking lot, not surprised when he followed her. "Probably wants to make sure I don't drive around the block and come back in five minutes."

So, where are you going to go now? Her practical side asked. To lose her escort, she would go home. Once the police officer stopped following her, she would figure out somewhere else to go.

Five minutes later she pulled into the driveway at the house. The police officer drove past and continued down the block, then out of sight.

"So, what now, Miss Smarty Pants?" she asked herself out loud.

Chapter 18

She waited for what felt like a lifetime, but by the clock on the dashboard had only been five minutes. As she waited, she studied the house she had lived in for the past ten years. The oversized, double paned windows were all dark. The big brick house was a tribute to Matthew and his success. To her it was a big, ugly brick box that had crushed her hopes and dreams and spirit as much as the man she had married.

Was Matthew still awake in there? Was he now regretting his actions? Probably not. He was never one to second-guess or regret anything. He had probably watched her drive away then gone to bed without any feelings one way or the other.

She would like nothing better than to never set foot in that house again, but understood that was hardly practical. She needed to be frugal, levelheaded and very, very practical. That meant returning to collect her belongings at some point in the not too distance future.

Starting the car, she backed down the driveway, but stopped dead in the middle of the street.

Where to now?

Putting the car in gear, she drove down the block. She was nearly a full block away before she turned on the headlights. With pain and exhaustion dulling her thinking, she drove to the only other place in town she felt comfortable.

She coasted to a stop in front of C&JJ Bail Bonds and flipped her headlights off and looked around. This house was dark as well. Glancing at her dashboard she understood. At 3:45 in the morning, the world slept. Taking a deep breath for courage and whispering a prayer that Cody would not appear waving a shotgun, she pulled down into the driveway and parked next to the company's big, black SUV.

She did not move for several minutes, waiting for lights, sirens and gunshots to shatter the night. But the neighborhood remained as silent and peaceful as it had been before her arrival.

Pulling her black BEA windbreaker from the floor of the back seat where someone had tossed her gear, she pulled it on backwards. After taking a long overdue pain pill, she settled in for a couple of hours of sleep. As her eyes slammed shut, she reminded herself she needed to wake up at 7:30 so she could go to McDonald's for breakfast before returning to her former home to gather her things. Hopefully she could pack her car and return here before nine o'clock. With that fervent prayer, she released her hold on consciousness and passed out.

* * * * *

She woke with a jerk then moaned as muscles and nerves she never knew she had screamed at her. She opened her right eye, but didn't move otherwise. Her left eye was so swollen it would not open. She was in her car. Swallowing, she moaned, then glanced at the dashboard. The tiny digital clock glowed 8:57. Pulling the handle of the her seat and shifting to allow the back to raise, she moaned again as pain slammed through the side of her face, then up from her left wrist.

Frannie Southerland. The emergency room. Matthew. The events of the previous day came back with startling clarity. Once she figured out where she was and why, she decided she needed to leave before one of the bosses caught her. Reaching for the ignition, she frowned.

Her keys were missing. She patted her pockets while looking around the front seat. Had she laid them on the center console? On the passenger's seat? In her pocket? No, no and no. The keys were nowhere to be found.

She jumped in surprise when the car door opened. "Looking for these?" Cody asked, holding her keys where she could see them.

"What are you doing with my keys?"

"Keeping you safe. Those painkillers you're on say you should not drive. What are you doing here anyway? I told you to take the day off."

Tears of embarrassment overflowed and she wiped them away with angry fingers. "My husband kicked me out when I got home. Said he doesn't want me anymore. I tried sleeping at Wal-Mart, but a policeman told me that parking lot was only for RVs. I had nowhere else to go so I ended up here about quarter to four." She could not keep up with the tears that were rolling down her cheeks in a steady stream so she gave up. The last thing she needed was a stuffed up nose.

"What are you going to do?" Cody asked, leaning against her car door so she could not close it on him.

"I'm going to get some breakfast, go to the house and pack my stuff. Then I'm going to the bank and take half of the money that is in our joint accounts. Then I guess I'm going to have to figure out where I'm going to spend tonight while I look for an apartment I can afford." She sounded more confident and in control that she felt.

"Sounds like a good plan, but I'll drive," Cody reached in and pulled her out of the seat.

"Don't you have to be in court today?"

"I sent JJ when I saw your car out here at dawn. I figured something like this might happen. Besides, with one arm in a cast, you're going to need someone to do the heavy lifting for you." Cody locked her car, then opened the passenger door of the SUV and helped her climb in. "Once we're finished with your list, I know of a place you can stay if you want."

"What's the rent on this place you know about?" she asked warily.

"Three hundred a month. And since I know where you work, I won't even demand a security deposit," Cody said, his tone almost warm and friendly. "It comes furnished if you want."

"Can I see it before I decide?" Three hundred dollars for a furnished place sounded way too good to be true. Was it a dump? Or was it a room just down the hall from his with midnight visits as part of the deal?

"Sure, but first we'll work through your list," Cody started the SUV and they headed out.

* * * * *

It only took an hour for her to pack her clothes then gather the pictures, quilts and other things she wanted from the house. Cody did not comment until after he had carried the two suitcases and two garbage bags to the car. "You want anything else?" he asked, skeptical as he looked around the rest of the house.

"This place used to give me nightmares. No, I don't think there's, no wait a minute." She hurried to the small half bath under the stairs and, using the empty trash can, collected everything in that room that was not nailed down. She tucked a hand towel around the top before carrying it to the kitchen.

"You know, you should strip the kitchen. After all, you deserve something for the years you've invested in this marriage. If you want, I can go back to the office and get my chainsaw and we'll take half of everything else with us, too." Cody smiled, but it was the smile of a feral cat on the hunt.

"No, I don't want anything else except those two books over there," she pointed to a pair of cookbooks next to the sink, "but to be smart, I probably should take everything in here. Matthew doesn't know how to cook."

Their next stop was the bank where Cody convinced her to clear the accounts of everything but one hundred dollars instead of just half. "He's getting the house and contents and that is not fair either," he pointed out when she argued that it did not seem fair for her to take all the money.

"I don't care. I just want out," she said, tired and in pain and just wanting to have this day over with.

"I know, but you're going to need more in the weeks to come," Cody pointed out as the teller counted the twenty-five $100 bills, all that was in their joint accounts.

Once they were back in the car, she laid her head back and tried to relax. When the SUV stopped and Cody turned off the engine, she struggled to open her eyes again. She looked around. The houses up and down the street were small, mostly brick with neat yards. They appeared well cared for, timeless, like they'd been standing here forever and would be here in another hundred years, still well loved and tended for.

She climbed out and turned to look at the house Cody was heading towards. She stopped mid step and caught her breath. It was the house she'd seen in her dreams when she'd been a child. A small house like the others up and down the street, but big enough for her. Red brick walls supported a tin room painted a complementary shade of gold. The porch and trim were the same warm gold and the shutters were deep green. The bushes were a little overgrown and the grass needed to be cut, but this was the house she had wanted since her eighth birthday when she'd found out that you could choose where you lived.

She followed Cody onto the porch and waited while he unlocked the front door. "This was my grandmother's house. The furniture's dated, but I've tried to keep it clean. If you need anything fixed, let me know and I'll take care of it," he said as he pushed the door open, then stepped back and waited for her to enter ahead of him.

She stopped on the porch, curiosity winning over common sense. "If this is your grandmother's house, where is she?"

Cody looked surprised for a moment, then smiled, but there was sadness in his expression. "She died about a year ago. She hasn't lived here in more than two years."

"I'm sorry," she said, embarrassed to her toes for being so nosy.

"Don't be, she lived a long, happy life and died doing what she wanted, playing golf in Palm Beach."

"Really?" Her eyes got big at the thought of an elderly woman keeling over on the twelfth green.

"Well, not exactly. She spent the day playing golf, then went home and during a nap she passed on. She had had a great round of golf that morning and was at peace with the world." Cody turned away, his voice growing tight with the memories. "Come on, I'll give you the nickel tour."

She crossed her fingers as she stepped over the threshold. Would the inside be as inviting as the outside? A moment later she decided it was even more so. The creamy white walls were bare. The sofa and chair covers were at least thirty years out of date, but she fell in love with the cottage.

Cody stood by the front door as she wandered through the two bedrooms, each furnished with double beds with shiny brass headboards, antique oak dressers and nightstands and a chair. One room had a rocking chair, the other a wingback chair covered with bright pink flowered fabric. In the kitchen she found the latest appliances and a huge, tawny, tiger-striped cat.

"Hello there," she said, kneeling and holding one hand out, palm down.

The cat rumbled a greeting and approached as if she was an old friend. He sniffed her fingers, licked one and then rubbed his head under her hand. He moved closer so he could settle his front feet on her thigh, raising himself closer. He continued purring, a loud, friendly sound. She rubbed his head for a minute, talking quietly to the friendly animal.

"That's Crazy Legs. He comes with the house, so I hope you're not allergic," Cody said, stepping into the room.

"No, I'm not." She straightened and was surprised when Crazy Legs circled around and around her, rubbing his side against her legs.

"My grandmother claimed he was a watch-cat. All I know is I can't get rid of him. Over the last six months I've given him away four times. He always shows back up here after a few days, hungry and demanding to get back inside."

"This is his home," she explained. "I love the house. Are you sure you can rent it so cheap?"

"It's paid for and you need a place. Besides, if you take care of Crazy Legs, you're doing me a giant favor."

Cody showed her where the cat food was stored and told her the cat's habits, likes and dislikes. He showed her where the sheets and towels were, the fuse box, thermostat and garbage cans. He worked one key off his key ring and handed it to her. He emptied the SUV and made sure the electricity, heat pump and water heater were all in working order.

"I'm going back to the office. Call me once you've settled in," Cody said when he finally left her

"Well, Mr. Crazy Legs, it looks like it's you and me," she said as she unpacked the bags of food, arranging the cans on empty shelves in the small pantry.

Crazy Legs rumbled his agreement, then wandered down the hall toward the bedrooms. She found him an hour later curled up on the pillow on the right hand side of the bed. After making the bed with clean sheets and her grandmother's quilt, she unpacked her clothes into the dresser and closet.

Only when her clothes and toiletries and food were neatly stored away and suitcases and plastic bags out of sight did she sit down and look around. Overwhelmed by Cody's kindness as well as the emotional and physical stresses and the amazing changes that had occurred in the last twenty-four hours, she burst into tears.

Chapter 19

The Sunday after moving into her new home, she woke early and planned that day's one brave thing.

Pushing Crazy Legs off the bed, she threw back the covers. "I don't have a Sunday dress any more, but I am going to church today. I'm even going to speak to people and try to make one new friend," she told the cat.

He rubbed against her leg and purred his approval. It never seemed to matter what she said, he always purred that rumbly noise that sounded like he agreed with her.

After putting food in his bowl and scrounging for breakfast for herself, she opened her closet and pulled out the first thing she touched. Tan slacks and a dressy white shirt would have to do. She dressed, then quickly brushed blush on her cheeks and a coat of mascara on her eyelashes. Clear lip-gloss and she was ready to go. Checking the clock by her bed, she picked up her purse and headed out.

The church parking lot was a third full when she arrived. She pulled in and parked, then sat there. She debated whether or not she should join the couples and families strolling toward the church or not.

Yes, she needed this. This was the next step in reclaiming herself and her independence. She no longer had to listen to Matthew or justify her behavior. Today she would go in that church, speak to people and try to meet women her own age.

With a deep breath for courage, she opened the door and climbed out. God was smiling on her this morning. Henrietta Simmons had just pulled in. The two women again sat together.

During the next hour, she relaxed and enjoyed the familiar traditions of the Methodist church service. She could feel the ragged hole in her heart begin to mend. As they left the church, her courage waned and she was tempted to slip from Henrietta's grasp and run for her car. But the older woman had a strong grip on her arm. As they left the sanctuary, Henrietta guided her towards a group of choir members in their navy blue robes. Henrietta seemed focused on a trio of women who looked about her age.

"Lacy, you all sang beautifully as usual," Henrietta hugged the brunette on the right.

"Thanks, Mama, but you always say that. Who's your friend?" Lacy returned her mother's hug.

Once introductions were made, she tried yet again to break away, but Lacy took over where her mother left off. "Come with me. I have to get out of this robe, then pick up my girls."

By the time she finally climbed into her car and left the church grounds, she had made three new friends. She'd also agreed to join them on Wednesday night for dinner at the church. She'd even given Lacy her cell phone number. She felt overwhelmed by their attention and friendship. She felt something she had not felt in a long, long time; that she was a person worthy of their friendship and love.

By the time she parked in front of her new home, she knew that she would be giving serious thought to Lacy's invitation to join the choir. She had not sung since high school, but Lacy assured that it did not matter, as long as she was willing to try and she had always loved to sing.

* * * * *

Over the next days, she spent her evenings making Cody's grandmother's house her own. After getting his okay, she hung photos on the walls in the living room. She visited the discount stores around town, buying pictures that caught her fancy. She bought bright, cheerful fabric and used her sewing skills to make slipcovers for the couch and chair in the living room and the chair in the second bedroom.

She turned the television on for company, but found herself spending more time talking to the cat than she did to herself. Maybe that was what she needed all along. A four-legged friend to talk to so she did not have to talk to herself. But Matthew refused to discuss getting any pet: dog, cat or canary.

Crazy Legs accepted her presence in the house easily. Whenever she sat down in the evenings, he would join her on the couch. He did not even mind when she got scared or blue or sad and cried into his fur. He just snuggled closer and purred in her ear. It was as if he was reassuring her in his own way that everything was going to be just fine. She was surprised at how easy the transition from married woman to separated woman went. She tried to keep busy so she did not have time to brood or worry about Matthew.

* * * * *

The Wednesday evening church dinner went well as she and her new friends, Lacy, Cynthia and Bridget grew closer. When she explained her living situation, the three were supportive and offered to be there anytime that she needed them.

The next evening she approached the choir room door

hesitantly. Would they let her join like this?

Before she could turn and make a run for her car, Lacy saw her and waved her into the room. Lacy joined her at the doorway and introduced her to Linda, the choir director, who then took over. In minutes she was assigned a choir robe and a music folder.

Then Linda asked the question she had been dreading. “Are you a soprano or an alto?”

“I was a soprano in high school, but haven’t sung since then,” she admitted, her voice tentative.

“Join Lacy in the soprano section and if we need to move you in the weeks to come we can. And welcome to the choir.”

“Thank you,” she said before following Lacy to their seats.

* * * * *

Two weeks later, she glanced up and down the hallway. No kids in sight. They were all caught up in their Wednesday night church activities. Pushing on the door marked “Women,” she stepped inside, bracing herself. The next few minutes were sure to be a test of the new friendships she had been easing into the last few weeks.

As she stepped around the door and fully into the rest room, conversation stopped. The three women already waiting there turned her way.

“Oh good Lord, what have you done to yourself?” Lacy asked as she stepped forward and enveloped her in a bear hug.

Before she could answer, Cynthia Fields pushed in and took over the hugging. “Did Matthew do this?”

She opened her mouth to explain, but Bridget Sheffield broke in. “I’ll get Joe’s shotgun and we’ll go teach him a few things about hurting women. Especially our new friend.”

“Whoa,” she said, taking a step back from the three women who were working themselves into a man-hating frenzy. “It wasn’t Matthew. He’s never raised a hand to me and I haven’t seen him since he kicked me out.”

"So how did you get hurt?" The three asked at the same time.

"Last night I went on another bounty hunter assignment. The woman I was supposed to contain and cuff did not want to be contained. She did this. Just some scrapes and bruises, but I was able to get her cuffed before Cody could swoop in and take over."

She filled her friends in on the last day and a half of her life and knew she had found true friends when they vowed to help in any way they could.

"Are you still doing your one brave thing a day?" Lacy asked.

"I'm trying, though I think yesterday qualified as my brave thing for the next month," she said.

"One brave thing a day? What's that?" Bridget asked, having missed their discussion the week before.

As she explained the OBTAD concept, Lacy looked thoughtful. "I wonder if that would work for my kids," she mused. As a high school guidance counselor, she was always looking for real world ideas and tools that she could use with teenagers.

"I don't see why it wouldn't work for anyone," she said. "It sure worked for me."

Feeling self-conscious with the focus on her, she turned the conversation to the projects the other women were involved in. Too soon children who were done with choir and ready to go home interrupted them.

* * * * *

She was surprised, yet not too shocked, when she did not hear anything from Matthew. After all, he didn't know where she worked, where she had moved to and probably the only thought he gave her was to wonder how to fix her spaghetti sauce on Monday nights. Two months after moving out, she arrived at the office to find JJ sitting in the conference room with a woman. The stranger wore an expensive navy suit, sensible heels, and discreet pearl earrings. Everything about her screamed lawyer.

"This is Vicki Rowen. She's the best divorce attorney in the county," JJ made the introductions, then dragged her into the hall just outside the conference room. He lowered his voice and looked straight into her eyes. "You probably haven't thought about it, but you need to file separation papers. Vicki's a friend and she really is the best."

"Thanks, JJ. I hadn't thought about it. You guys are too good to me," she said, amazed that this man with gentle eyes and what could be a frighteningly fierce expression could be so thoughtful.

"Hey, you've been a Godsend. We've done more business with fewer skips since you hired on than in the five years we've been in business. We don't want to lose you." JJ patted her shoulder, then pushed her back into the conference room.

"JJ tells me you need to file separation papers," Vicki Rowen pulled out a file and opened it.

"Yes, my husband threw me out two months ago and I want to get a divorce," she said aloud for the first time. A weight the size of Oklahoma lifted from her shoulders as she acknowledged the reality of the situation and her decision out loud for the first time.

For the next half-hour she answered the questions the attorney threw at her, feeling more and more certain that this was the right thing to do. Leaving Matthew was one thing; divorce was the logical next step. She would never return to living the way she had and knew he would never change. He couldn't. He was a man.

In the time she had been on her own she discovered that she was stronger than she could ever have imagined and did not want to lose the strides she was making toward becoming independent and self-sufficient.

After finishing the forms, Vicki asked one last question. "Will we need to file for a restraining order? Your husband won't try to hurt you when he gets these papers, will he?"

"No, I don't think he'd do that, though he might try to find me to talk about it, which might be just as painful," she said.

Vicki nodded as she repacked her briefcase. "I'll call here when the papers are ready to be signed. Once you've signed them, we'll messenger them to your husband for his signature. Then we'll file them at the courthouse. After a year and one day you will be able to file for divorce. Just remember that if you and your husband spend even one night together, the clock kicks back to zero and you'll have to wait another year and one day before divorcing."

She nodded. "I don't plan on seeing him so that's not a problem."

"You might be surprised." Vicki said. "I'll be in touch."

She showed Vicki out, then returned to her desk, feeling a surprising lightness in her soul. Filing the separation papers was today's big brave thing. It might even qualify for tomorrow's as well. The backbone she thought had been missing was thickening each day, growing stronger and stronger. With it, her self-esteem was rising and she was becoming more and more like the girl she had been in high school—bold, brash and in charge.

I am strong and smart and important. I am good for something. I can do this.

Chapter 20

She sat at a table for four, the only person eating alone in the family restaurant that evening. In a show of strength, she decided not to share that today was her birthday with Cody or JJ, but instead took herself out for a fancy meal. The hostess had situated her at a table in the back, the table no one ever wants to sit at. This table was an after thought and really did not have enough room. It got bumped every time anyone went in or out of the kitchen.

The staff moved so quickly past her that she did not have time to complain or ask for a seat somewhere, anywhere, else in the room. She could have eaten at the bar, but that felt like she was giving in to the aloneness. There were no other tables to be had. In fact, the waiting area was getting crowded as people kept coming in and no one left.

As she sat there, she examined every detail of every picture on the walls and tried not to eavesdrop on the conversations going on around her. She made a mental note that, from now on when dining in a restaurant alone, she needed to bring a book or magazine, something to take her mind off the fact that she was alone.

"Stop it," she ordered herself softly as she dropped her gaze to her empty plate. "You have just as much right to be here as anyone else." She closed her mouth when the busboy who was on his way to the kitchen gave her a look wondering if she were crazy.

You're allowed a nice meal in a nice restaurant, especially on your birthday.

It wasn't her fault that she was still sitting here fifteen minutes after she'd finished eating. Her waitress had disappeared and not come back, though she had asked for her bill. She would get up and leave, but she did not want to, not yet. She wanted to stay a little longer amongst people, even if they were strangers.

When the clapping started she looked around, her heart thumping in fright. Did someone know it was her birthday? No, the staff was headed away from her. The leader of the merry band carried a piece of pie with a lit candle in the center. She watched as they sang the required birthday song to a blushing middle-age man. A round of applause from everyone in the room finished the birthday tribute. She looked down at her empty plate and wished for a single moment that someone knew it was her birthday. But she'd told no one, so how was anyone to know?

"So, how was everything?" A voice barked. It was the thin, teenage waitress with over-processed hair, too much makeup and piercings in odd places in her face. She was finally back from her break. No, this wasn't the same girl. This was her near twin with the addition of a gold hoop through her left nostril.

"It was fine, thanks," she answered in a squeaking voice that sounded like that of a nervous child.

"Would you like dessert?" The waitress asked, already bored with this customer and ready to move on.

"No, I'm still waiting for my check," she said, disappointment shafting through her, shattering the triumph of her brave act for the day. She had come alone to a restaurant and now she was scurrying out like a frightened rabbit. She had to get over this. She was allowed to live and breathe and go out to eat a nice dinner out just like everyone else.

The waitress nodded and took her dishes, disappearing into the kitchen without another word. She was left studying the crumbs on the tablecloth. The longer she sat there, the angrier she became. She should not have to put up with this kind of neglect. Pushing to her feet, she walked to the front of the bar and waved for the bartender. From watching the room for the last hour, she knew he also the manager on duty.

"This should cover my tab. I've been waiting twenty minutes for my waitress to bring my check and I'm leaving now. Good night." She handed the man a twenty, then turned and walked out.

Her anger burned away halfway home. Then she realized that by standing up for herself she had taken yet another brave step on the path toward being strong and bold and maybe even a little outrageous in this new life of singleness she was embracing.

* * * * *

Thursday morning, Vicki Rowen's office called. The papers were ready for her signature. Five minutes later, when Cody appeared in the office doorway, she was stunned. For the first time in their association, he not wearing a black T-shirt and military cargo pants. Instead, he was wearing a burgundy dress shirt and khaki slacks with deck shoes. Dressed in black he was formidable. Dressed like this, he was enough to take any woman's breath away.

"Wow," she murmured, turning to her computer so he wouldn't see her drool. After all, one sure way to die of embarrassment was by throwing herself at his feet and begging him to do with her as he pleased. What was happening to her?

"What's up?" she asked, scanning the calendar to see if he had any appointments that called for such dressiness.

"Your separation papers are ready to be signed. I thought you might like someone to go with you," he said.

"You don't have to do that," she said, her throat thickening at this man's thoughtfulness. "How did you know? Ms. Rowen's office called me just a few minutes ago."

"She called JJ first. He called me. We thought one of us should go with you, just in case."

"I'll be fine. It's just a couple of signatures and then I'll be done. You didn't have to get dressed up to go with me."

"Come on, I'll drive," Cody said.

"You know, sometimes I feel like I'm making great strides. Other times I feel just as spineless as I ever was with Matthew," she muttered to herself as she followed Cody down the wide hall.

The SUV was unusually silent during the eight-block drive to Vicki Rowen's office. The closer they got, the tenser she became. All at once she was not so sure about what she was doing. She had not spoken to Matthew in the eight weeks since his parents' anniversary dinner. She was half surprised that he had not come looking for her or contacted the papers about his missing wife. Some act to prove he felt something for her.

Cody escorted her into the lawyer's office, one hand just barely resting in the middle of her back. The warmth of his palm was a protective comfort. The woman sitting in the reception area was the epitome of what she imagined a good office worker should look like. She wore an expensive looking navy suit with a silk blouse and stylish gold jewelry. Her make up was understated; her artfully streaked blonde hair cut in a chin length bob. She felt frumpy and inferior wearing chinos and a black Henley with the company logo over her left breast.

"Good morning, may I help you?" the woman asked with a polite, friendly smile.

"Someone called that my separation agreement is ready to be signed," she stepped forward, immediately missing the support of Cody's hand.

"Yes, I just finished printing it out. Please read this over and if everything is correct, you'll need to sign all three copies. We'll messenger them to your husband this afternoon for his signature. Hopefully we'll have the signed copies back early next week and then we'll file them at the courthouse. Would you prefer to pick up your copy when it's ready, or have us mail it to you?"

"Mailing it would be great," she said. She accepted one copy of the document, settled in a comfortable club chair and began to read. Cody settled in the chair opposite her and waited. He never moved as she read through the seven-page document. Once she finished, she carried the papers back to the reception desk and signed all the three copies under the watchful eye of the receptionist.

"Thank you," she said before turning and following Cody back out to the SUV.

"You okay?" Cody asked as they headed back to the office.

"I'm not sure. It all feels like a dream. Matthew will probably freak out when he gets those papers."

"He might. But he might just sign them and go on. Hard to say."

"Yeah," she said, turning to look out the window.

But he won't. He'll want to talk, complain and demand an explanation as to why I screwed up his precious bank records. And who will cook for him and clean for him and be there when he's horny?

Once they were back at the office, Cody turned to study her. "Why don't you take the afternoon off. Go to a movie, go shopping, do something fun for yourself."

She smiled sadly. "Funny how men always suggest spending money when a woman's broke. I'd rather be at work doing something productive. Otherwise I'll just go home and worry that I've done the wrong thing or how I'll react when Matthew shows up at my door."

Cody stared at her for a long moment before nodding. "Okay, work it is. But JJ and I want to take you to dinner tonight to celebrate."

"Celebrate?"

"Yeah. You've taken giant steps in your bid for independence. But we want to celebrate your promotion and raise. You've been officially promoted to office manager. And with this promotion comes a raise."

"This doesn't mean I'll be buying dinner, does it?" She cocked one eyebrow.

"No, the company's buying dinner and drinks. So wrap your mind around getting drunk and sharing all your secrets," Cody said with a smile that looked friendly and wolfish at the same time.

Chapter 21

Just before midnight, she stared hard at the doorknob. She squinted, trying to decide which of the three keyholes to aim for. At least she had thought enough to turn on the porch light when she returned home earlier to change clothes. Trying to do this in the dark would have been impossible.

The bright porch light and an excess of alcohol kept her from seeing the sporty car parked two houses down on the opposite side of the street. But the driver watched her with an intensity she would have felt had her senses not been numbed by one too many Bahama Mamas. JJ and Cody swore the drink was harmless. Earlier she would have agreed. The fruity combination of pineapple and orange juices masked the kick ass strength of the alcohol.

After a round of miniature golf which, surprisingly, she had won thanks to four holes-in-one, they dropped JJ off at the courthouse to bail out one of their regular clients and Cody brought her home. Only now the alcohol was blurring her vision and had loosened her joints so her knees wobbled and she wasn't sure she was standing exactly straight.

"Need some help?"

She heard a tone in Cody's voice and frowned. He was amused at her condition. At least he was not criticizing her for being drunk. That thread of suppressed laughter steeled her determination. "No, thanks," she muttered. She would open the door without any help from him or anyone else.

Deciding the process of elimination would be easiest she started by stabbing her key at the keyhole on the left. But the key didn't slid into the tiny slot. Clenching her jaw even harder, she tried the one on the right. Again the metal key hit the wooden door.

So why didn't you start with the middle one?

Instead of answering herself, she poked at the keyhole in the middle. But at the last second, her whole body shifted and she missed the knob with the key, instead smashing her knuckles against the door. "Owwww," she cried, lifting her hand to her lips and stabbing herself in the chin with the key.

Tears sprang to fill her eyes. She had been doing so well. But here she was, beaten by a door. How could a door defeat her determination to be a strong, independent woman?

When Cody plucked the key ring from her hand, she did not argue. She had no fight left. Taking a step sideways, she allowed him access to the door, silently admitting her resignation to being assisted by a man. At least this man did not criticize her actions as he helped her.

Cody had the door unlocked and pushed open in two heartbeats. Taking her hand, he led her into her own house. The living room light was on its lowest setting and he looked around with interest. This might have been his grandmother's home at one time, but she had made it her own.

She had repainted the walls a soft peach color that seemed to glow in the lamplight. The family photographs that had once crowded the walls had been replaced by a few prints of famous paintings he vaguely recognized. Even the furniture, while being the same, was different with new burnt orange canvas covers and bright red, blue and yellow pillows.

"The place looks great," he said when he realized the silence between them had gone on for too long.

"Thanks. It was fun to make this place my own. I've never had my own home before," she said, sounding sad even to her own ears.

Cody closed the door and led her to the couch. He pushed her down and began to worry when she collapsed onto the seat without argument, refusal or even a dirty look in his direction. She was well and truly drunk. Maybe now he could get answers to the questions that had been eating at him ever since he'd hired her.

"Tell me about your husband," he said. He settled at the opposite end of the couch, leaving more than a foot of space between them. He turned slightly, allowing an easy view of this sad lady. He was not sure she could make it to the bathroom without help if she needed to be sick. She had done such a great job with the house he did not want her to mess it up.

"Matthew is a sweet-talking, two-faced, controlling bully. He has to be in total control of his world. His job, his house, his wife. No one should ever get his in way or else..." she lapsed into a reflective silence.

"Did he ever hit you?" Cody asked gently.

"Oh no. He didn't have to. His words caused enough damage. Once upon a time I wanted to do something with my life, be someone important. I wanted to help people, make a difference. I wanted to have lots of friends and lots of children and three dogs running around," she spoke softly, her words slurring lightly.

"Then I met Matthew. I thought he wanted the same things I did. After an intense six months of seeing one another almost every day, he decided we should get married. I was just uncertain enough of myself to agree. Only after we were married did I learn that in public he was sweet and charming and attentive. In the privacy of his own home, he wasn't quite so nice. Over the last few years, I've become a living, breathing doormat who knew better than to try and make decisions on my own."

"Why not?"

"My decisions were always wrong or so he claimed. My choice of friends, clothes, food, the job I had when we got married. He cut me off from the friends I had before I met him. He kept me from going out and making new friends. I've lived in this town for ten years and the one friend who won't let Matthew bully her into abandoning me lives a thousand miles away. If I died tomorrow no one would come to my funeral," she admitted. The inhibitions and fears that had kept her silent for so long had washed away with the alcohol of the evening.

"I'd come. I'd miss you," Cody said. He brushed a lone tear from her cheek.

She blinked, frowned and tried to focus on the man beside her. With the lamp behind him, his face was in shadow so she could not read his expression. "Thanks. I appreciate that. Don't let anyone put roses on my grave. Wildflowers in every color of the rainbow, okay?" she said, leaning slightly into his touch.

"No roses. But we shouldn't be talking about this right now. You're going to live to be a very old lady with dozens of friends and children and grandchildren around you, filling your world with love."

"Yeah, right. All I have to do divorce Matthew and find a man who is everything my husband isn't. A man who will want me for me, as I am and not for the potential I might or might not be able to live up to."

"You'll find him. He's out there. But first you need to get to know who you are and what you want out of life. It's hard for someone else to love us if we don't love ourselves first," Cody said, shifting three inches closer.

"But how do I do that?"

"Start by forgiving yourself. You made a mistake marrying Matthew. Admit it and forgive yourself. Then move forward.

Learn what you like and don't like and figure out how you want to spend the rest of your life."

The simplicity of what he was saying made sense, but also saddened her even more. In a handful of heartbeats she was sobbing.

"Ah, it's not so bad." Cody closed the distance between them. He wrapped one arm around her back and pulled her close.

She didn't respond. She was too busy feeling sorry for herself. He held her loosely, but provided a security she had not felt since snuggling with her mother on stormy afternoons when she was a little girl.

Trying to control her tears, she straightened from where she had somehow ended up lying across his chest. She averted her eyes, not wanting to read condemnation in his expression.

But he would not let her escape so easy. "Look at me," he ordered in a gentle tone. He cradled her chin between thumb and forefinger to keep her from turning away.

She wanted to pull away, to turn and run, but the gentle order had her raising her eyes and staring into his. She saw no disappointment there, no anger or criticism. What she saw was warmth and concern and something else. Something she could not define.

"What do you see?" Cody asked in a gruff whisper.

"I...I'm...not sure," she answered honestly.

"What you see is a friend. Someone who cares about you and wants only the best for you," he said, his voice growing deeper and rougher with each word.

She took a breath, then another. No one had ever admitted to being her friend before. No one had ever wanted to be her friend for very long after they met Matthew. Not that he was rude or mean to them. He usually turned on the acidly sweet charm, while knocking her down with every word he said. His behavior made others uncomfortable so they would drift away.

Cody would stick by her. Although if Matthew met him, he might try to convince her bosses that she was crazy. Cody, on the other hand, would probably punch Matthew in the nose.

"Hey, where'd you go?" he asked, brushing a strand of hair from her cheek.

She did not answer him. Instead she leaned forward and brushed her lips over his. "Thank you," she whispered against his lips.

Cody pulled back first. "You're welcome. Now let's get you to bed so you can dream about friends and children and animals."

He was rejecting her, but that was okay. Truth be told, he scared her. Men in general scared her. Or maybe it was just that she was frightened of herself and her need for a man to lean on. She allowed Cody to release her and push to his feet. She followed suit and found that since sitting on the couch, the bones in her legs had dissolved.

Before her knees hit the floor, Cody grabbed her and pulled her into the solid trunk of his body. "Whoa there. No sleeping on the floor." He took a step sideways then shifted, bent and scooped her up, cradling her like a child in his arms.

"Wow, how'd you do that?" she asked as he carried her across the living room and down the hall.

"Strong man secret," he said. He smiled over her head at the childlike wonder this woman had for the most mundane actions of life.

"Oh, well, that's why Matthew never did this for me. He's not strong," she said, beginning to giggle again. "He always said it was because I was too fat."

It took ten minutes to get her settled into the bed. She spent most of that time debating the merits of nightgowns over pajamas. Finally she cooperated long enough to change into the oversized T-shirt she claimed was her nightgown.

When she slipped under the covers, she wiggled her way across the mattress and settled on the left side of the bed. "Good night, Cody," she murmured as she slipped into alcohol induced sleep.

"Good night, sweet dreams," Cody said flipping off the light.

He turned and almost tripped over Crazy Legs. "Damn cat, where do you think you're going?"

After staring at him for a full fifteen seconds, Crazy Legs brushed past him with a rumbly purr and flick of his tail. The overweight cat marched into the bedroom and leapt up to the bed. He walked across the mattress and nuzzled its occupant, licking her ear until the unconscious woman brushed his nose with a "Good night, baby. Go to sleep."

With that, Crazy Legs climbed onto the pillow on the right side of the bed, circled twice and flopped down. His considerable bulk covered most of the pillow.

"Good night, cat. Keep her safe. She's a special lady." With that Cody pulled the door half-closed and left the woman and her watch-cat to their dreams.

After turning off the lights in the living room and front porch, Cody stepped out the front door and made sure it locked when he pulled it closed behind him. He was tempted to crash on the couch, or in the second bedroom, but knew she would not thank him for that. She would be hurting in the morning and probably embarrassed that she let barriers down in front of him. Better to give her time to recover from her hangover and maybe think about what they had talked about. That is, if she even remembered what they talked about. Hard to believe that one woman would get so smashed from only three drinks.

Heading to the SUV, for the first time since high school he was unaware of his surroundings. He did not notice the car two houses down and across the street was now gone.

* * * * *

Just after dawn the doorbell rang three times in rapid succession, jolting her from sleep. She sat straight up and moaned when her head and her stomach revolted at the rapid movement. Then pounding on the door began, matching the thumping in her head as she threw off the covers and raced to the bathroom.

After throwing up, she rinsed her mouth and brushed the nasty tasting fur from her teeth and tongue. She grabbed the bottle of over the counter painkillers and headed for the living room. Pulling a pair of navy blue sweatpants off the doorknob of her bedroom, she stopped long enough to pull them on. Then she headed to the front door.

The pounding continued. It stopped when she threw the dead bolt. "Thank God," she murmured as she twisted the lock in the knob, then opened the door. She didn't bother using the peephole. It was too small and distorted things beyond recognition. Besides, it was probably Cody or J.J. Hopefully they had a Pepsi with them. She needed sugar and caffeine and she needed them now.

She squinted against the early morning light that streamed into her eyes. Her headache ratcheted up another notch, forcing a groan from her. Focusing on her visitor, she groaned again, then swayed on her feet as her world shifted.

"What the hell do you want?" she growled.

Chapter 22

"What the hell have you done?" Matthew answered her question with one of his own. "You've ruined yourself!"

She frowned as Matthew stared at her as if he could not believe what he saw. Then it hit her. He was having a hard time with her appearance. Not only had she been losing weight and shaping up, she done the one thing she knew would make Matthew crazy.

The Tuesday before as her daily brave thing, she had gotten a haircut. For the first time in ten years she did not just trim her bangs. An 18-inch ponytail of hair had been bundled, braided, cut and donated to Locks of Love, an organization that provided wigs for children who had lost their hair due to illness.

Before cutting off the ponytail, the stylist turned the chair so she could not see what was happening. The woman then snipped and combed and styled. All the while she talked about what wonderful hair she had and how cute and easy this style would be compared to her waist length tresses. When she was finished, the stylist spun the chair back around so she could see the final result. She could not believe the change. Her hair was super short, spiky and moved when she shook her head.

What surprised her most was that her eyes were now the focal point of her face. They were no longer dead pools that provided sight. They had begun to sparkle again. What had once been flat, dull, blah brown now glinted with gold flecks, deep and full of life.

From the hair salon, she went to the mall and learned how to apply and wear make up and how to take proper care of her skin. It had cost a small fortune, but she felt more feminine than she had in years.

Matthew crossed his arms and cleared his throat. He looked more like her disapproving father than ever before. She ran one hand through her hair, combing it as the stylist shown her. "I got a haircut," she stated simply.

She would have shaken her head to fluff her hair, but it hurt to breathe. Shaking her head might kill her. "What do you want, Matthew?" she asked, leaning a little more into the doorframe and wondering how much longer she would have to stand here squinting into the morning sun.

"I thought I could come in so we can talk about those papers," he said, clearly not happy with the changes she'd made in the past weeks.

She took a deep breath to stay strong. This was the moment she had been dreading since signing the papers the previous day. "What's to talk about? You threw me out. I filed for divorce. My lawyer is demanding a full accounting of income, expenses and investments made and where the money is now that you claimed you had been saving for our retirement. There is nothing else for us to talk about." She shifted to close the door, but he took half a step forward and blocked her.

"You're my wife. You can't do this. I won't let you. Who was that gorilla you brought home last night? You'll never hold onto him. He's not so dumb that he won't see that you're not woman enough for him."

She tried to think past the pain thumping at her temples. Last night. Drinks. Mexican food. Cody sitting on her couch. Waking up this morning.

"How do you know about last night?" she asked.

For the first time in years she looked, really looked, at the man she had once bound her love to. He, too, was older, and thicker in the middle. The muscular upper body he had been so proud of had deflated leaving him with sloped shoulders and a sunken chest. His hairline had receded and what was left had grown dull and limp with silver threads starting to become more noticeable. His skin, though tanned from weekends fishing, had an almost yellow appearance to it due to the beer he drank more and more frequently over the last few years.

"I was here when you two came home last night. Who the hell is he?" Matthew spit at her. He shifted and pulled his foot back so he had a more solid stance.

She grinned as she said, "Nunya. Go away Matthew. Don't come back. You don't want me. You don't like me. I'm not sure you've loved me in a long time. I've just become a habit. Divorce is the best thing for both of us."

Her words, spoken in a resigned tone, caught him off guard. He looked at her for a long moment before stepping back. "You'll be back. You'll never make it on your own. No one else will want you. You'll come back to me." He continued muttering to himself all the way down her walk.

She remained in the doorway, not relaxing until he drove away. The smile blooming in her heart grew. A minute later she was standing in the doorway in her nightshirt and sweatpants grinning like a half-witted fool. She'd done it. She'd faced him down. She had accomplished the biggest bravest thing she could.

Closing and locking the front door, she raised her arms, screamed and began a two-stepping happy jig around the room. Crazy Legs meowed in protest and ran for the kitchen door, well out of way of her dancing feet.

You just don't appreciate the situation," she told the cat as he flicked his tail at her and disappeared down the hallway. "This is a momentous occasion. The doormat not only grew a backbone, but teeth and claws as well."

A few minutes later, the explosive joy of her accomplishment drained away and she was left feeling shaky and unsure. Guilt and fear washed over her as well.

Could he be right? Would she return to him? How was she to make it on her own?

Pushing all the uncertainty away, she focused on the positive. "You'll do it just like every other divorced woman in the world. One day at a time, one hour at a time if need be. And you will not be afraid to ask for help when needed and to reach out to others whenever necessary," she assured herself.

Though her head thumped with hangover pain, she pulled on her exercise clothes and forced herself to do her calisthenics and then walk two miles. After a long, hot shower, she ate breakfast, then headed to the office.

She was unsure what to expect when she saw Cody and tried to prepare herself for anything. He was in the office restocking the court briefcase when she arrived.

"Morning," he said as he zipped the case closed. He sounded no different than he had any other morning when faced with court.

"Good morning," she said. Even to her own ears she sounded too chipper.

Cody looked her way, cocked one eyebrow, but did not ask the question that was obviously on his mind.

He was headed out the doorway when she swallowed hard. "Did anything happen last night that I should be mortified about? Other than kissing you, that is?" she asked, her voice soft and tentative.

He turned in the doorway. "No. But I don't think you should get a tattoo, no matter where you're thinking of putting it." He grinned at her expression of confused horror. "Don't worry. You did nothing to be ashamed of, not even that kiss." Before she could respond to his teasing, he ducked out the door.

* * * * *

On her lunch break, she took her cell phone and went to the front porch. She dialed a number she'd called several times over the last months.

After two rings, the phone clicked. "Coalition Against Family Violence, this is Jane," came the answer.

For the next twenty minutes, she caught Jane up on what had been happening, including the separation, her new home, her haircut and that morning's dawn showdown with Matthew. Jane listened, congratulating her and whooping with joy in all the appropriate places.

"Would you come to our support group and share your story? We need more women like you to share their triumphs and let others know that it is possible to overcome a situation such as yours." Jane asked when she finally wound down.

"Yeah, I could do that. When and where?"

* * * * *

Monday evening she pulled into the parking lot and looked at the half dozen other cars in the lot. Suddenly she was nervous. "One more brave thing today," she said as she climbed from her car and entered the building.

A woman met her outside the door, introduced herself and looked tense until she explained she was there for the meeting and that Jane had sent her. Then the woman smiled and the walls came down. A few minutes later that same woman called the group to order and began by laying out the rules of the group and then had everyone introduce themselves, saying that they had a special guest tonight who wanted to share with them.

Once introductions were made, she shifted in her chair as all eyes turned her way. The six other women stared at her with interest, with wary caution, with fear. All emotions she could identify with. After all, they had all experienced the same things, an abusive and controlling relationship. Closing her eyes, she took a breath and began. “My name is Samantha Morgan and this is my story...”